D.G.'s voice suddenly rang out. "Freeze!"

Two dogs—Doberman pinschers—trotted around the bend and stopped in the middle of the road, staring at them. Everett's heart leaped and he caught his breath. Dobermans were the worst. Everyone stood statue still.

Tina edged over next to Everett. "Should we run?" she whispered.

"Stand still," Everett said. "If we run, they may come after us."

D.G. slowly reached to his back pocket and pulled out his sling. The dogs continued staring. D.G. whispered out of the side of his mouth. "Get a stone ready, everyone."

Holding his breath, Everett inched his hand up to his pocket and drew out the slingshot as furtively as he could. Then he grabbed a stone.

Suddenly, the dogs were up and barking, still hesitating about what to do. Tina turned to run. Linc followed. Everett wanted to run, but he knew he couldn't desert D.G. Then with a loud double bark, the dogs leaped forward. The dogs were less than a hundred feet away now. Tina shouted, "Run!"

ADVENTURE AT ROCKY CREEK

Mark R. Littleton

Chariot Books™
David C. Cook Publishing Co.

Chariot Books™ is an imprint of David C. Cook Publishing Co.
David C. Cook Publishing Co., Elgin, Illinois 60120
David C. Cook Publishing Co., Weston, Ontario
Nova Distribution Ltd., Newton Abbot, England

ADVENTURE AT ROCKY CREEK
© 1993 by Mark R. Littleton

Cover design by Bill Paetzold
Cover illustration by Nathan Greene
First Printing, 1993
Printed in the United States of America
97 96 95 94 93   5 4 3 2 1

Library of Congress Cataloging-in-Publication Data
Littleton, Mark R.,
    Adventure at Rocky Creek / by Mark R. Littleton.
        p.   cm.
    Summary: Branded a yellow-belly coward and shunned by his former friends because
he ran away from a fight, eleven-year-old Everett gets a second chance to prove himself
through prayer and the discovery of an abandoned house being used by robbers.
    ISBN 1-55513-761-X
    [1. Courage–Fiction. 2. Christian life–Fiction. 3. Robbers and outlaws–Fiction.] I.
Title
PZ7.L7364Ad   1992
[Fic] –dc20   92-8047
                                                 CIP
                                                  AC

Contents

1
What Happened behind the Shopping Center

Everett could tell by the way Chuck was talking, there was no getting out of it this time. O'Brien wanted a fight.

"So let's give it to him—right?" said Chuck as he looked from Everett to Stuart. He jerked his head to the right, flicking his straight brown hair farther up his forehead.

Stuart nodded and said through clenched teeth, "We can take O'Brien and his little mascot, Mullen." The three of them headed up the street, with Chuck talking big and Stuart and Everett hurrying on either side of him. Everett told himself there was nothing to fear, but inside he worried about O'Brien. He was big and mean. He'd flunked once or twice so he should have been in seventh grade. And he played dirty.

"Okay, we've got to have a plan," Chuck went on. "He's pushed us around too much. So this time we deck him. We take him fast and hard. No messing around." Chuck threw punches into the air as he walked.

Everett shook inside his denim jacket. The air smelled of mown grass, but something in the back of his head reminded him of the odor of blood. His whole body jumped and jolted like a racing engine. He had never been in a fight before, not a real fight. Not where each side wanted to hurt the other.

Everett bunched his fist and shot a quick jab.

Chuck grinned at him. "That's it. Fast and hard."

Everett glanced at the bigger boy a moment and smirked. It would be all right, he told himself again. He was proud he was Chuck's friend. Chuck Davis didn't let just anyone be his friend. Though he wasn't the most popular kid in the fifth grade, he had class, guts, courage. They'd all moved from different places into a new housing subdivision called Sparkton Homes in New Castleton, New Jersey. Chuck was the oldest—twelve. Everett and Stuart were both eleven. All three of the boys were the oldest kids in their families.

"All right, I'll call the shots," Chuck said. "I do the talking, got it?"

Stuart and Everett both nodded.

"If O'Brien comes at us behind the shopping center, we

move quickly. Suddenly. Like Pearl Harbor." Chuck was well built for his age, with a thick chest and arms. He always won arm wrestling matches with the others.

Everett clenched and unclenched his fists, wondering what would it feel like to be hit, hit hard by someone like O'Brien. For keeps. O'Brien played for keeps. He wanted to hurt you and hurt you bad.

Everett raked his curly blond hair across his forehead.

Chuck warned, "If O'Brien gets dirty, we get dirty right back."

"We can take him," Stuart said. He was skinny but hard as a knothole from playing midget football in the fall and swimming in the summer. He brushed his fingers through his dark, straight hair and made a nasty face. He had hard blue eyes that Everett always found difficult to look into.

Everett coughed. For a second, he wondered why O'Brien got so mad about them coming out behind the shopping center. O'Brien hung around the trucks back there, and once Everett had seen him hauling something out of one of them. He suspected O'Brien was a thief in addition to being a bully.

His mouth was dry. Everett wondered deep down if he was the wimp Chuck had said he was. One time, when he wouldn't drink one of Mr. Davis's beers or look at his *Playboys*, Chuck had said he was a "religious freak." It bothered him.

"We have to have some signals," Chuck added, making muscles. "Let's do it this way. If I shout 'Let's go,' then we lay into him. If I shout, 'Burn,' we run. But I'm not yelling 'Burn' unless O'Brien's got a knife or something."

Knife or something!?

The words hit Everett like a jab to the jaw. A *knife or something?* He hadn't counted on anything like that.

Chuck gave him a sudden, piercing look. "You chicken out on this, Abels, you're out. You understand?"

Everett answered tightly, "I'm not going to chicken out." But his eyes blurred and the queasiness in his stomach sent convulsions through his abdomen. He figured he could take Mullen, the little guy who hung with O'Brien. But his temples pounded. It felt like someone stood at his side and hit him in the head with a hammer.

They reached the shopping center and wound around behind it to the sidewalk. That would bring them out at the far end, between the drugstore and Bink's.

"If O'Brien doesn't show," Chuck said, "we keep coming back till he does. Right?"

O'Brien didn't appear behind the shopping center, so the three went on to the drugstore and bought Cokes. The Coke tasted flat. Everett's tongue felt as though it were covered with sand. The flashy colors in the store came at him like sound blasts.

Chuck and Stuart finished their Cokes and crunched the cans with both hands, then heaved them into the trash bin. Everett dumped his in still half full. He tried not to look into Chuck's eyes. He hated the way Chuck kept looking at him.

As they headed toward the exit, Chuck said again, "Anyone runs, they're out. No more club, no more motocross. Out. Got it?"

Everett didn't answer. He searched the path ahead for signs of O'Brien. No one was in sight. Stuart jammed his hands into his shorts pockets and said, "We're gonna nail him."

They came around a corner. O'Brien, smooth as a whiplash, jumped out in front of them. "Well, if it isn't the Bobbsey Triplets," he said with a sneer. "I don't suppose you guys would want to buy a knuckle sandwich or two, would you?"

Mullen postured slightly behind O'Brien. Cigarettes dangled from their lips. O'Brien's thick black hair looked greasy as it swept across his forehead.

"Lay off, O'Brien," said Chuck. "We're not taking any more stuff off of you." Chuck took a stolid stand about ten feet in front of O'Brien and motioned to Everett and Stuart to spread out to his right and left. *Just stay cool*, Everett told himself.

O'Brien tried to get between them and the path to block off their exit, but Chuck danced around to keep it behind them.

Everett repeated the words in his mind. *Let's go. Burn.* That was the signal.

O'Brien stepped forward, jabbing, then curling up like a prizefighter. "Come on, Davis, let's see your stuff."

Chuck hesitated. He stepped back, and Everett and

Stuart instinctively stepped back with him. Chuck glanced uneasily at Everett. "We don't want to hurt you, O'Brien." His voice was shaking.

"Hurt me? Don't you have it mixed up, box brain? You're the ones who'll be hurt."

Mullen swayed toward Everett, his eyes slit with a mean glow. Everett tried to concentrate. But his knees were shaking so badly he thought he would fall down. He kept his hands up, curled into fists.

"I'm telling you, O'Brien, you don't want this," Chuck yelled. He glanced at Everett and Stuart. "Should we give it to him?"

Everett felt his face prickling. He tried to steel himself. Where was the signal?

Mullen darted toward him, then stopped, watching Everett's face for a sign of fear. They were about five feet apart. "Come on, jerk brain, hit me."

Everett waited. *Give us the signal, Chuck!* Were they supposed to run or fight?

His mind blurred and he blinked. Mullen leaped at him. O'Brien lashed at Chuck. Instantly, Everett saw the pipe, carefully covered up in O'Brien's fist. A shout came into his throat.

Chuck roared.

The signal!

Everett shrieked, "Pipe!" then wheeled and bolted for the path. His legs burned with pain as he stretched for as much ground between steps as possible. He heard the slap of sneakers on concrete and he pushed harder. In several seconds he reached the fence by the back of the shopping center.

Just make it to the street!

He sprinted around the curve and down the sidewalk to the houses beyond. Seconds later he reached the first driveway.

"Man, I thought we were going to get creamed," he panted as he turned, almost ready to laugh. "O'Brien had a pipe. I was afraid . . ."

But when he turned around, he stood there alone.

2
Break

"Oh, no! Oh, no!" Everett yelled and froze. "Chuck's gonna . . ." He sprang forward. He had to get back before it was too late.

As Everett ran, his mind exploded with terror. There had to be some mistake. Hadn't Chuck given the signal? Hadn't he shouted, "Burn!"?

When he reached the parking lot, Chuck was on the ground and so was Stuart. Both of them were bleeding. Everett ran up to them. "What happened? I thought . . ."

Chuck jerked around, holding his nose. Blood dripped through his fingers. Stuart had a cut lip and his eye looked swollen. Chuck screamed, "You coward, Abels! You yellow-belly chicken!"

Everett stared, his heart hammering inside him. Chuck started to rise, then sank back down in pain.

"I'll call the police!" Everett said, swallowing. He glanced around for signs of O'Brien.

"Just get away from me," Chuck said angrily and stumbled to his feet. Stuart followed him, dangling his arm and holding his jaw. They walked past Everett, glaring at him with hard eyes.

Everett breathed hard, trying to think of something to say. "I thought you gave the sig—"

But they walked on, not turning around.

As he stared after the two, bent over, hobbling up the sidewalk, scenes from the past flashed into his mind. How Chuck had been so angry over a baseball card trade Everett wouldn't agree to, and how he'd given Everett the silent treatment for nearly a week afterward. How Chuck had made fun of him once in front of some of the other boys when Everett hesitated about skinny dipping in the creek. Chuck's words had stung. "He's probably really a girl."

Everett knew this time it would be worse, much worse.

For a moment, he wished O'Brien would hurtle back out of the bushes and beat him up. He stood there for several minutes, breathing hard and trying to clear his mind. But the fear inside him was like a wrench tightening a little nut. In a moment, it would snap.

When nothing happened, he finally lurched forward,

terrified now at what Chuck would do. He tried to tell himself, "It'll be all right. It'll work out." But deep down he knew it might be days—or weeks! Maybe more. Maybe forever.

When he stood at his back door, he could barely remember how he'd gotten there. It was a mistake, he told himself. It was a mistake. He thought Chuck had given the signal. He'd seen the pipe. They had agreed, hadn't they? Hadn't Chuck shouted?

Angry tears burned into Everett's eyes as he climbed the stairs to his room. He heard his younger sister Jillie and brother Lance arguing in the family room. He didn't want to see them either. He knew he'd never live this down. Everyone in the school would know. Chuck would make sure of that.

Everett crumpled onto his bed, trying to get his breath. "Why did this have to happen?" he murmured.

The words echoed inside his mind. Yellow-belly chicken! Everett cringed and tried to lie still.

As he brushed angrily at the silent tears, Everett thought about all the things he and Chuck and Stuart had done together since he'd met them after moving to New Castleton. His room was studded with the mementos: a Phillies pennant, some Cub Scout patches, a game-winning baseball.

He didn't make friends easily. His own family had moved three times before they'd come to New Castleton. Each time they'd lived in apartments. There weren't many kids around. And the ones who were kept to themselves. Everett had found himself a loner.

But when Chuck came to the neighborhood, he roared in like a hurricane. He was so full of energy. They built forts together in the backyard, up in the trees. Together they would set up Chuck's horde of army men, lay them out on the basement floor, and shoot them down with rubber-band guns. Chuck taught Everett and Stuart poker, hearts, Crazy Eights, Monopoly. They played marathon games. Sometimes they all stayed overnight in Chuck's room or camped out and drank Coke and ate popcorn till the late hours. Chuck had legions of baseball cards and always gave Stuart and Everett his extras.

Everett curled up, gripping his knees, trying to think of where to go, what to do. He wished somehow he could suddenly be someone else, or turn into a bird and flutter away. He just didn't want to be Everett Abels anymore.

He lay back and stared at the ceiling, a darkness pressing on his chest. The next thing he knew his mother was waking him up for dinner.

That night, Everett walked determinedly over to the Davis's house to see Chuck and try to patch things up. Everett wasn't sure how he could explain it to Chuck, but he knew he had to, or they'd never be friends again.

"You have to make it right as soon as possible," his father had advised. "You can't let something like that sit."

Mr. Davis met him at the door and greeted him

cordially. "Sure, go on in, Everett. He's in the family room."

Everett stepped inside. His heart was so loud in his chest, he suddenly felt dizzy. Stuart and Chuck were watching a movie. Both of Chuck's eyes were black, and he had a huge bandage over his nose and across his face.

The moment he saw Everett, his lip curled and his face darkened. "You traitor, Abels! You yellow-belly chicken! How dare you come in here?" He started to stand, but when he did, he suddenly crumpled over in pain, his face twisting. He screamed as he fell back. "Mom!"

Mrs. Davis rushed to the door.

"Who said he could come in here?"

"But Everett's your best fr—"

"Not anymore. I don't want to see him."

Everett felt as though he was pinned underwater. His neck felt tight and his face damp. Somehow he managed, "I'm sorry, Chuck, I thought you said . . ."

"You thought! You thought!"

Both of Chuck's parents now stood in the doorway.

"All you thought about was your own yellow-belly hide."

"Chuck!" Mr. Davis said. "That's enough."

"I don't want any coward in my house." He gave Everett a surly glance and hunched over, pressing his temples.

"You need to calm down, boy," Mr. Davis said coolly.

Chuck stared at his father, then began to rise toward Everett. "I ought to punch you out myself. In fact, I think I will." He lunged at him, but Mr. Davis stepped between them, catching Chuck in his arms.

Chuck cried out with pain. "My nose!"

"That's right, your nose," said Mr. Davis, pointing Chuck back to the couch. "Now sit down. Don't you think you've been in enough fights today?"

Chuck staggered to the couch, holding his hands up to his face. He cried, "It hurts, Mom. It really hurts."

His mother quietly sat down next to him and took his hands away from his face. "You're not supposed to move around, honey. Or talk loud—remember?"

Chuck glared at Everett. His eyes were wet. "You always were a yellow belly. I should have known we couldn't trust you. I just should have known."

Everett's lips quivered. He felt exposed, naked, as if everyone else had clothes and he didn't. "Chuck, I'm sorry. I didn't mean . . . Please forgive . . ."

Chuck's eyes burned with anger. Everett could feel him saying the word. *Yellow belly.*

Everett bowed his head and swallowed.

Yellow belly!

"Look, I think you'd better go, Everett," Chuck's father finally said. "I'm sorry about all this."

"He's just upset," said Mrs. Davis, guiding him to the door.

As Everett turned to go out, Chuck called after him. "Believe me, I don't want you coming back here."

Everett hung his head and screwed up his lips, trying to hold back the shriek of pain that seemed to be winding through his body. Somehow he walked to the doorway to go out.

Mr. Davis lay his hand on Everett's shoulder. "Don't worry about it, Everett. Chuck'll get over it. It was just a mistake."

Everett didn't answer. As he walked out, he felt as though the whole world knew he and Chuck were no longer friends. He could hear the laughing in his mind. "Abels? You mean the yellow belly?"

A sob heaved up through his chest and into his throat.

When he stepped through the back door and into the family room, his father looked up from the paper. Lance and Jillie were watching television and his mother studied some needlework. Everett hurried by on the way to his room, but his dad called him. "How did it go, Ev?"

The boy stopped and said mechanically, not looking at anyone, "We're not friends anymore, that's all." He bit his lip and started up the stairs.

"It'll be okay, honey. It will," his mother said, standing and laying down the needlework.

She put her arm over his shoulder and nudged him. "Maybe we should pray a moment?" She glanced at Mr. Abels and he nodded, then got up.

Everett waited, thinking, *What good would that do?* Still, he let her pray, barely listening to the words.

When she was done, he just felt dark. And tired. Like his life was over.

3
Yellow Belly

"**I** hear you chickened out," Jesse Olford remarked to Everett when he slunk into his classroom that Monday morning, trying not to be noticed.

Everett glanced at a group crowded around Stuart, laughing and snickering. He said, "I guess that's what people are saying."

"Is it true?"

True?

He walked to his seat without saying anything. Jesse followed him.

"Is it true you ran and left Chuck and Stuart to face O'Brien?"

Everett stowed his books inside the desk. The little group around Stuart waited in silence. Everett felt every eye on the side of his cheek. The room was dead quiet.

Everett sat down slowly, telling himself just to ignore them.

"Well?" Jesse put his hands on his hips. "Come on, Abels. Answer."

Everett shrugged, trying to look as if it didn't bother him. "Ask Stuart," he said through tight lips.

"Stuart already told us his side. What's yours?"

Couldn't the guy just lay off? Everett pulled out a book. "I'm not talking about it."

"So you did run, didn't you?"

Everett forced himself to look at the words on the page, but he couldn't read them. A buzz filled his mind that choked off all thought.

Then Mrs. Gibbs walked into the room and banged her ruler on the desk. "Everyone in their seats."

Class began and Everett breathed a little more easily. But he could feel the glances and hear the whispers, the little snickers from different parts of the room.

Chuck came back to school in the middle of the week. He didn't say anything to Everett. Three or four times, Everett tried to speak with him alone. But somehow Chuck always made sure he never had a chance. He would turn and march the other way when he saw Everett coming, or begin talking to someone nearby, even if they weren't friends.

Everett tried to think of something he could do to prove it was all a mistake. He was sure he ran only because he thought Chuck had given the signal. But in reality he couldn't even convince himself of that now. Maybe he was a wimp. And a coward.

That Friday, the gym teacher asked Stuart and another kid named Harris Malkin to choose up for a game of softball. Chuck couldn't play because of his broken nose, so he watched. Everett stood on the baseline as the players were selected. Normally a captain picked him in the first three or four choices.

This time no one chose Everett. He kept blinking his eyes, fixing them on the dirt in front of his feet.

In the end, Everett played on Stuart's team. Right field. No one spoke to him, though, even after he hit a triple.

During the last month of school, Stuart and Chuck continued to give Everett the silent treatment. Chuck had his usual group of friends around him, with Stuart acting as though he were the prince of the planet.

Everett tried desperately to come up with something to do to gain their respect. But he couldn't think of anything, and nothing happened that might make it possible.

In the middle of May, he received a letter about joining Little League. He knew Chuck and Stuart should have received the same letter, and they would be on the same team. That night Everett's father spotted it on the dining room table.

"So what do you say, Ev? Are you going out?"

Everett had thought about it all afternoon. "I don't think so," he said with a shrug.

His father gave him a long look. "I'm not going to force you, Ev. But I think it would be good for you."

Inside, Everett knew he was right. He decided not to fight it and went out the first night of the tryouts. Chuck and Stuart were there. They said nothing to him. But the way they snubbed him made him feel low and cold inside. Twice when he batted, he heard Chuck make snide remarks. When he bobbled a grounder at third base, he noticed Chuck looking at him with that sarcastic curl of his lip. It was then he knew he couldn't take a whole summer of that.

At home that night, he announced he was quitting. His father adjusted his glasses, but his mother said, "You can't avoid them for the rest of your life, honey."

"I know."

"Then why don't you stick it out?"

"Because maybe they're right."

"About what?" his father said.

Everett swallowed. The words caught in his throat. *Yellow belly*. Suddenly, he turned and ran upstairs, flopping on his bed and staring at the wall.

A minute later, his dad stood by his bed. "Ev?"

"What?" Everett didn't turn around.

"Whatever you decide to do, we'll be behind you." He felt his father's hand on his shoulder.

"I'm not going out for the team."

"All right. But do you have good reason?"

Everett sucked the edge of his lip. Why did he have to have a good reason? Why couldn't it just be he didn't want to?

He didn't answer. Finally his father squeezed his shoulder and sighed. "Everett, you have to make your own decisions. I don't think this is the best one, but I'll go along with it for now."

Tears slid into Everett's eyes. *Why did this have to happen? Why?* He thought of God, of prayer, of things he'd learned in church. That God works all things for good. That God loves you. That God is in control of everything.

Well, if He was, where was He? Why didn't He fix this thing?

"I'll be here when you want to talk," his father finally said, then turned and went out. Everett lay in the dark for a few minutes trying to figure out what he should do.

He rolled over and listened to the sounds of the evening. There had to be something he could do to convince Chuck he wasn't really a coward and that they could be friends again. But it seemed impossible. No one, not even God, could fix this.

4
D.G.

Everett lay in bed and gazed out the window. School finished a week before. The sun shone brightly on the thick, green grass like a welcome mat. It was the first day of summer, June 21. He could play baseball or basketball. He could swim at the local swimming pool. He could go running. But what he wanted was a friend. Just one. He knew Chuck wouldn't budge, and Stuart wouldn't change so long as Chuck wouldn't. So he knew he had to do something on his own. He gritted his teeth and threw the sheet off his legs.

"All right. That's the way it is," he said, brushing his

teeth with angry jerks. "Then that's the way it is. I'll live."

He regretted not going out for the Little League team, but there was another league in the subdivision, a father/son league that Chuck always put down because they didn't wear regular uniforms. Everett's dad talked him into joining it. It turned out to be fun. He met some new kids, blasted a few hits and made several remarkable plays. The kids on the team seemed friendly enough, but he didn't meet any that seemed to want to be friends outside the league.

After dressing, he peered out the window to the clearing beyond the backyard where a new elementary school was being built. That spring the Barckley Construction Company had begun building more houses down the street from Everett's house. The farm that once bordered their property was halved, with new houses lining the streets. Behind the Abels's home men on bulldozers had cleared out the woods to build the school. Everett would attend there in the fall, if they finished it in time.

Behind the school now were towering mounds of trees cut down and piled high like prickly mountains.

Everett picked up his baseball glove and ball. He'd take them with him, anyway. He could always find a wall somewhere, chalk on a strike zone, and pitch balls at it. "So what if I don't have anyone," he said out loud with a kick at his bed. "I can take it."

The moment he said it, his mother called from the kitchen. "That you, Evvie? You're up early." It was nine o'clock.

He padded over the linoleum bricks into the kitchen with his mitt in his hand. "Didn't feel like sleeping in."

She riffled his hair, but he stepped back. He loved his mother, but he didn't like her treating him like a little boy.

"Playing some ball today?" She fixed her gray, quiet eyes on him and smiled.

"I guess so."

She didn't ask the obvious question: "With who?"

"What do you want for breakfast?"

"Whatever."

She gazed at him affectionately, pinched his cheeks, then turned to the stove, brushing the blonde bangs out of her eyes.

He knew that look—that penetrating, "I love you and I'll help any way I can" gaze. But he didn't want to act all sad and unhappy about it. If he didn't find someone, he didn't find someone. That was that.

But he already felt tired and edgy.

He could feel her worrying over him as he slumped at the table. He knew very well what she probably wanted to say. "Pray about it. The Lord'll bring you somebody."

That always killed him. *The Lord.* She was always talking about the Lord. Like He was really there watching him. What did He care about Everett Abels? If He really cared, why had He let him run? Why had God let Chuck dump him? His mother was always saying He'd do this, He'd do that. Well, why didn't He just do it and be done with it?

He was spared any more looks from his mother when eight-year-old Lance and seven-year-old Jillie shuffled in.

Through the curtains, the day looked warm and inviting. Everett felt more positive after scarfing down a plate of scrambled eggs. He announced that he was going out to explore the mounds behind the house. Jillie said, "I want to come with you."

But Everett frowned and glanced at his mother. He was definitely tired of Jillie's doll games where he had to carry on fake conversations with little stuffed animals about dumb things like what your name was and how old you were.

His mother commented, "Jillie, Evvie has to explore on his own a little."

"But he's only played with me about two minutes."

Two minutes my eye, Everett thought. *More like a month—straight.*

"Everett, you do need to give Jillie and Lance some time too," his mother said. He hated it when she gave him that sweet, please-help-out look.

"I'll play a game with you later," he said.

"Barbies?" she squealed. "Will you play Barbies?"

He nodded. "After lunch." At least he didn't have anyone like Chuck standing around to give him a good, "What a wimp," talk about it.

Chuck. Why couldn't he just get Chuck out of his mind?

But he couldn't. If Chuck and Stuart had been there, they would already be pitching and hitting their way through a World Series whiffleball game. Or down in the woods, carving sticks into snakes. Or trying to catch fish in Peters Lake. Or . . .

A moment later, he got up and rushed out of the house, forgetting to bring his baseball glove and ball.

On the way across the rough, stump-strewn field, he decided to explore the tree dumps behind the school. There were always construction workers around the school, and he stayed away from them. The chug of bulldozers and other huge machines kept the air buzzing. But Everett traipsed to the far end of the mounds and began climbing in among them. The pungent aroma of garbage, tar, and fresh-turned dirt filled his nostrils. The sun was warm on his face, and his blue T-shirt was already damp with sweat.

The tree trunks, limbs, and broken building materials were piled in a disorderly mishmash that Everett soon discovered was fun. He could climb in among them, even hide. He wondered if he could make some kind of fort out of the materials, lodge it deep within a mound, and create his own secret hideaway.

But as he crawled in and out of the gnarled trees and junk, he suddenly heard another boy's voice.

"Fix your sights, sergeant. Ready? Aim? Blast 'em." A pause. "Boom! Another tank decimated by the Israelis!"

Everett sank down behind a pile of tree trunks and listened.

"Two more tanks coming up on the left, sir. The Golan

Heights are for the taking if we can blow them over."

"Do it, commander."

Not sure whether there were two voices, or one person making two voices, or even more, Everett peeked out from behind a log. Were they kids from school? How many? Chuck wasn't with them, was he?

He peered over the edge of a smelly stump and tried to locate where the sound was coming from. It seemed to come up right out of one of the mounds.

"Acka, acka, acka—the Uzi automatic mows down a squad of Arabs! Boom! Boom! Two shots and the tanks are smithereened."

"We've got the heights, General."

"General Moshe Dayan shifts the patch over his eye and stares out over the battlefield."

"We shall have *shalom* tonight, he says. It's been six days and the war is almost over. We've conquered. Just like David and Goliath."

Everett listened with fascination. It couldn't be more than two, but it sounded like one person speaking all the parts.

Then suddenly the voice changed. "I'll take him, sir. He may be nine feet tall, but my sling can get him." He watched as a boy shorter than he leaped up onto a tree trunk. He had a tousled brown head, dark eyes, and a maroon sweatshirt that said PENN STATE. Then Everett saw the birthmark. The left side of his face was a red splotch. Everett's heart sank. He knew who this guy was.

D.G. Frankl. In one of the other fifth-grade classes, they called him "Scarface," though not usually to his face. He was kind of a loner. But Everett had never really spoken to him before. He was also on one of the other teams in the father/son league.

Suddenly, D.G. began whirling something around his head. Moments later, a pebble dinged into a trunk nearby and bounced off into the dirt.

"Hey!" shouted Everett without thinking.

There was a sudden silence. The boy disappeared.

Everett waited. *Should I stand up?* His heart began to pound. He listened intently. Nothing but silence. Finally, he squinted over the edge of the trunk. Then he stood up. "Hey! You could hurt somebody with that."

The boy peered out suspiciously over another tree trunk about thirty feet to Everett's left. He hesitated, gazing at Everett uncomfortably. Then he said, "Do you come for peace or for war, sir?"

5
The Tank

Everett clambered carefully onto the tree trunk.
"Peace, I guess." He chuckled at the strangeness of D.G.
He'd heard about a lot of the weird things this kid did. If
Chuck knew he even gave Frankl the time of day, he'd be
laughing in his face. But for the moment, that didn't
matter. At least it was something to do. For awhile, or at
least until something better came along.

There was another long pause while the boy studied
him. "Okay," he said with squinting eyes. "Approach with
hands up." He shook the leather thong in his hand and
watched. The birthmark appeared crimson in the hot

sunlight. Everett noticed his armpits were wet.

But he stepped over a tree trunk and several pieces of twisted metal. A moment later, he found he couldn't keep his hands up or he'd slip.

"I'll fall down if I keep my hands up. Can't I put them down?"

D.G. shrugged. "Okay, just don't go for your Uzi."

Everett knew that was some kind of Middle East weapon. He'd read about them in the paper. "I don't have one," he said. Man, was this kid for real?

D.G. snorted. "Everybody has an Uzi."

Everett let his arms drop and hiked over the pile to where the boy was standing. In a moment, they faced one another. D.G. was about three or four inches shorter than Everett, and bonier. He had brown hair, curly and uncombed, that seemed to go every which way. Hanging in his right hand was the leather thong with a pouch in the middle. He wore blue jean shorts, the maroon sweatshirt cut off at the sleeves, and running shoes. D.G. stared into his face. "You're Everett Abels."

Everett nodded. "Yeah. And you're D.G. Frankl."

There was a long pause while D.G. looked around nervously. Then he turned and gazed deeply into Everett's eyes. D.G. had sharp, deep brown eyes that seemed to see right through you. It made Everett feel nervous. But he wasn't going to be afraid of this kid, even if he was supposed to be weird.

"So do you want to drill some Egyptians with me?"

There was a hopeful tone in his voice that Everett noticed, as though he wanted you to agree, but wasn't going to beg you about it.

Everett nodded sheepishly. D.G. was better than no one, even if he was supposed to be strange. "Sure." He remembered how D.G. batted in baseball, all crouched over and that birthmark flaming on his cheek like some kind of badge.

D.G. grinned suddenly. "All right, you'll be the gunnery sergeant. Would you care to inspect my tank? M-60. American made."

Everett glanced down into the tangle of tree branches, trunks, and clapboard. There was a cavelike hole under the top logs, and he could see some tires and carved sticks lying about.

"Um, where?"

"Right here."

D.G. led him down into the opening. As he entered, Everett realized D.G. must have been working on the thing for several days. The sunshine cut through the cracks between the branches, so there was no problem seeing. The shade made it feel cooler.

The inside of the tank was about four feet square with several flat boards making a bottom area and branches sticking into the main space. The ends of a number of logs were sheared flat, and Everett noticed a saw leaning up against the side. Some sticks with notches and electrician's tape hung on pegs on one wall. There was also a broken caulking gun and several other tools probably thrown away from the construction site. Another pile of logs with sharpened tips lay against the other side. In the middle perched a black piece of pipe on a little stumplike stand.

"My gun and my shells," said D.G., pointing to the pipe and then the sharp-tipped logs. "105 millimeter. We're getting low on ammunition. Wiped out eight Egyptian tanks today." D.G. stared at him again, searching his eyes, as if he were waiting for something to happen.

Everett turned his gaze on a small bike tire with a nail driven through the hub into a tree trunk.

"That's how we steer," D.G. said. "That's why the Arabs keep losing. We have better maneuverability. Plus . . ." he pointed to his head, "Israeli brains. Brain over brawn. Wins every time." He set his chin in a strange way, sticking it out, as though he were waiting for someone to hit him.

"What're all these?" Everett pointed to the racked sticks with the black tape.

D.G. pulled several down. "Colt .45 blowback sergeant's side gun. AK-47. Russian. Captured from a dead Arab. And this," he said proudly, "is my Uzi. Best all-round weapon there is. Accuracy to fifty yards. Over ten rounds a second. Can tear apart a cinder block wall with one 32-shell clip."

Everett looked around and almost wanted to laugh. He had to admit it was cool. "How did you make all this stuff?"

D.G. pointed to his head again. "Israeli brains. Remember, brains over brawn. That's what wins wars. Take it from Moshe Dayan."

"Who's that?" Everett said absently. He didn't remember reading about him in the Bible.

"The greatest general in Israelite history," D.G. said with a confident nod. "Recent history, that is. Others are Joshua, King David, and Jehoshaphat."

Everett was sure now that D.G. was Jewish. He'd never had a close Jewish friend, so he thought it might be interesting getting to know him.

Suddenly Everett caught himself gazing at D.G.'s birthmark. He knew kids at school really razzed D.G. about it. D.G. had a slight build. No one thought of him as a tough kid, so it was easy to put him down.

He looked at the leather thong still dangling from D.G.'s hand. "And that—what's that?"

For the first time D.G. smiled. It was a wrinkled, sly kind of smile, bent up on the right side. "This is my slingshot. David the King used one to slay Goliath."

"Seems it can really whip one at you."

"Definitely," said D.G. "I'll show you." He lay both ends of the thong in his hand, grabbed a pebble from the floor, settled it in the pouch in the middle of the thong, and began climbing out of the tank. A moment later he stood on the top trunk. He whipped the sling around his head. Everett was about to jump up, but D.G. yelled, "Stay down." Then, "See that piece of white board over there?"

Everett squinted and saw the board about twenty feet away, lying against some branches.

D.G. let the stone fly. It smacked the board in the upper

left-hand corner. D.G. turned and shrugged. "Not as accurate as an Uzi." He paused. "That is. Not yet."

As D.G. swaggered back down into the tank, Everett wondered what "D.G." stood for. He couldn't help but stare a moment at D.G.'s birthmark again as D.G. bent to pick up another stone. When he looked up, D.G. suddenly said, "That's my birthmark."

Everett nodded uneasily. "I know."

"Do you want to see it up close?"

Everett was surprised at D.G.'s directness. Everett said, "It doesn't bother me." He knew it was a lie.

But D.G leaned forward. "Go ahead, look at it."

Swallowing, Everett scrutinized the birthmark, although he suddenly felt shy and embarrassed. Bright red jagged lines came out from the center blotch like a fireworks explosion. Briefly Everett felt sorry for D.G. Then he realized D.G. didn't feel that way about it.

The boy said, "It won't hurt you. My mom says it's where the angel kissed me."

Everett smiled uneasily. He'd heard that expression before.

"But it was really a congenital infection, when I was in the womb. My dad says it's the way God made me special, so my dad would be able to pick me out in a crowd anywhere."

Nodding again, Everett tried to act as though it were all right.

"Yeah, it's all just to make me feel better about it."

The way D.G. looked at him made Everett feel bad. "It's okay," he said, "everybody has something that's different about them."

D.G. brightened. "Right. I knew you wouldn't mind. Not like . . ."

He didn't finish the sentence.

Everett decided it wasn't so bad. After all, he had a birthmark on his belly and sometimes felt a little embarrassed when he went swimming. He figured he wasn't going to make a big deal about it. It wasn't like D.G. could help it. Anyway, it wasn't as though he were going to spend the whole summer with him.

"Some kids call me 'Scarface' in school," D.G. added.

Man, this kid didn't pull any punches, did he? He said, "Do you like that?"

"No." There was a determined look in D.G.'s eyes. He said, "You won't call me that, will you?"

Everett winced again. How could he be like that? "No, I'll call you D.G." *If I ever see you again,* he thought.

Grinning, D.G. said, "Should I call you Everett or Ev or what?"

Everett watched as D.G.'s dark eyes brightened happily. *This kid was really serious. He wanted to be friends. Well, what did it matter? It was only for one day.* "Yeah, Everett's fine. Just call me Everett."

He suddenly remembered how Chuck had once made fun of his name. "Sounds like a battery that went dead." Everett hadn't liked it, but Chuck was always cutting down people about the way they walked, the way their nose curved, the way their eyebrows came together, all kinds of crazy things.

D.G. gave him another long look, then glanced at his feet and cleared his throat. "So you want to be friends?"

Stifling a laugh in his throat, Everett hesitated, then nodded yes. But he thought, *What on earth have I gotten into?* He knew what Chuck thought of D.G. Frankl. If he got to be friends with D.G., there would be no end to the put-downs. But still, D.G. was so sincere.

D.G. said, "Well, maybe we can just be acquaintances for the moment."

"Acquaintances!" Everett said with a chuckle. "You sound like a teacher or something."

D.G. shrugged. "It's better than nothing." His face was still serious, but Everett could see the hurt in his eyes. It stung Everett a moment, but he knew there was no way he could be friends with him the way he'd been with Chuck. Not permanent friends. Be seen with one another at the shopping center and places? Ha.

"It's all right," D.G. said. "I understand. I'm the class weirdo." There was a hint of hopelessness in his voice that cut Everett to the heart. Yet, it wasn't as if D.G. wanted him to feel sorry for him.

Suddenly, without thinking, Everett said, "It's okay. I want to do this. It's fun. Don't worry about it."

Instantly, D.G. smiled his triumphant smile. "What else can anyone ask for?"

He paused and looked around. "Okay, you ready to deal some shells to the Arabs?" D.G. led him back down into the tank.

Everett chuckled and said, "What do I do?"

D.G. showed him how the tank worked. He shoved a shell into the pipe and flipped a door he had taped to it. Then he pretended to aim, shouted, "Fire!" and made a gravelly KAPOW sound. Everett was soon feeding the barrel shells, steering the tank, and fighting the enemy.

That morning, D.G. kept up a running monologue of all the events that were happening. Everett realized it all had something to do with a war between the Israelis and Arabs, but he didn't know what. The only war he knew about was the one that had been against Iraq in the Middle East. And Israel wasn't in that one.

They destroyed some forty-two tanks, wiped out eighteen platoons of foot soldiers—"grunts," as D.G. called them—and captured hundreds more. By the time they were done, it was twelve o'clock. A siren went off up near the highway.

Shielding his eyes from the noon sun, Everett said, "I'll have to go home for lunch."

"Do you want to come back tomorrow?" D.G. gave Everett an optimistic look, and Everett knew he couldn't say no.

"Sure. Nine o'clock?"

"Got it."

But Everett wasn't sure he'd really come. Only if nothing better came along.

Looking away toward his house, Everett suddenly turned and looked at D.G. "So what does D.G. mean?"

D.G. looked away with a frown. "My initials."

"Right." He paused, then rubbed his sneaker toe on a tree trunk. "But what do they stand for?"

D.G. jumped up and began to walk across the pile of trees toward his house. "Someday I'll tell you," he called over his shoulder. "Special intelligence information. Not for public consumption." He gave Everett his confident smile again, and then it suddenly faded. He said with a shrug, "They stand for Dodai Gamaliel. Two great men of Israel. My mother wanted Dodai because that's her grandfather's name; my father liked Gamaliel." He bunched his lips up, then said, "But most people—some, I mean— call me, D.G. That's what I prefer."

He flashed that bright look again and Everett nodded. "I'll call you D.G." Everett smiled. "Thanks for telling me."

As D.G. walked away, Everett had a distinct feeling it was not something he told everyone.

That night Everett saw D.G. at the baseball game. His team played after Everett's game was finished. He ran up to Everett with his glove in his hand. "I didn't know you played here."

Everett answered quickly. He wasn't sure he wanted other kids to see him talking to D.G. "Yeah. We won tonight. Anyway, I have to go."

D.G. beamed. "All right. See you tomorrow." He gave

him his crinkly smile and the birthmark on his cheek seemed brighter than ever. Joining his father, Everett walked quickly back toward his house, hoping no one saw him talk to D.G. His dad was talking about the game, but Everett didn't pay much attention. He wondered if he really should come back tomorrow. He would feel bad about not showing up. What had his mother told him? "You always keep your word." He supposed it was in the Bible somewhere. But did God expect him to be permanent friends with someone like D.G.?

He decided not to think about it. D.G. did seem like a nice-enough guy. He wasn't completely weird. And anyway, everyone was a little weird in some way. But what would he do if he ran into Chuck and Stuart with D.G. there?

As they reached home, he heard his dad say, "I see you're making some friends."

Everett hurried in. "Yeah. A few."

That evening Mr. Abels said to Everett, "Do you know anything about some robberies that have happened in the area? They say the shopping center was robbed. Right out of the trucks in the back."

Everett remembered seeing O'Brien there. "Not really."

"Well, be careful. You still go up there now and then, don't you?"

"Sometimes."

"Apparently, they think some local thieves have been robbing the trucks overnight. They're saying some kids might be involved."

Everett thought about saying something about O'Brien. But he decided that couldn't be. O'Brien was still only in fifth grade. He turned back to watching television. "All right, Dad. But don't worry about me."

He kept thinking about D.G., whether he should really be friends with him.

That night when he went to bed, Everett said to his mother, "Mom, were you ever friends with someone other kids didn't like?"

She laughed at his question, then said, "I think I've always been friends with people others didn't like."

"Really?"

"Evvie, I don't think there's a person on the face of the earth whom everyone likes."

"But why don't people like each other sometimes?"

She sighed and brushed his hair back with her hand. "I suppose it's because we don't love one another the way we should. If we loved the way God says we should, we'd never be able to hate anyone."

"Maybe if the person was perfect, others wouldn't hate him."

She shook her head sadly. "No, Jesus was perfect and plenty of people hated Him."

Everett thought for a minute. "Yeah, I guess you're right about that."

She gazed at him thoughtfully. "What, did you meet someone today that other kids don't like?"

"Sort of."

"Who is he?"

"A kid in one of the classes."

"Do you like him?"

Everett screwed up his face. Why did she have to ask that?

"Well, do you like him?"

Finally, he shrugged. "I don't know, Mom. He's different."

"How is he different?"

Everett was beginning to regret the whole conversation. "I don't know, Mom. I'm going to sleep."

Before he rolled over, she touched his shoulder and made him look her in the eye. "Give him a chance, honey, whoever he is. You might be surprised. Some people you don't know how to take turn out to be the greatest friends in life."

"How do you know that?"

"Because that's how your father and I started out."

"Oh, Mom, that's not . . ."

"It's true, honey."

He shook his head. "I'm going to sleep."

But as she left the room and switched off the light, he thought about it. "God," he prayed, "don't let me do the wrong thing again. That's all I ask."

In another five minutes, he was asleep.

6
The Jackal

Everett spotted D.G. approaching the tank before D.G. saw him. Everett had arrived early just to look around. He hadn't decided even to come until that morning, but he was bored with Jillie and Lance and wanted to do something different. At least with D.G. he could be sure of doing something different.

D.G. ran up to him eagerly. "I guess we're still friends, huh?"

Smiling, Everett tried to work up some real enthusiasm in reply. But D.G. didn't wait for an answer. "Come on, I'll show you the coolest thing," he said as he turned to race toward the school.

Everett hesitated.

D.G. turned around.

"You're not afraid, are you?"

"No."

"Where are we going?" Everett didn't want to get into trouble.

"Over by the space station."

"The space station!"

"The school. But I call it the space station." He glanced around and lowered his voice. "It's been taken over."

Everett looked toward the school. He thought this was getting to be some kind of baby game, but he played along. "By who?"

"Some kind of aliens," D.G. said. He looked hard into Everett's eyes. "Look, I know it's just a game, but lighten up, okay?"

Everett still felt uncomfortable being with D.G.

Impatient for an answer, D.G. suddenly threw out his hands. "Okay, what do you want to do? We don't have to do what I want to do. What do you want to do?"

Everett didn't like the way D.G. looked at him, like a puppy who suddenly didn't understand why you were being mean to him. Shifting his weight and swallowing, Everett tried to think of a logical answer. But D.G. blinked and looked away, his face suddenly showing a hint of anger. "All right. I won't bother you. I just thought . . ." He started to walk away.

"No, D.G., wait a minute. I'm sorry. I just don't . . ."

Everett jumped off the log and hurried after the smaller boy.

But D.G. whipped around. His birthmark was crimson and he was obviously angry. "Look, if you don't want to be friends with me, you don't have to, all right? I can take it. I can live with it—all right? I'm not going to act like you're the last person on earth." He turned and marched away.

Pausing only a second, Everett scrambled after the boy. "D.G. I didn't mean it. I . . ."

D.G. turned around again. His jaw flexed and unflexed. "All right, let's get one thing straight then."

"What?" Everett swallowed and stopped.

"I know a little about you being great friends with Chuck Davis and Stuart Coble. And then you weren't friends anymore. I don't know why, but it doesn't matter to me, okay? I believe what I see, not what I hear, okay? So if you're going to be friends with me, you'll have to go by what you see, not by what you hear. Understand? With me as well as you."

Everett swallowed and shifted his weight. He moved his eyes up until he was looking directly into D.G.'s. Everett slowly put out his hand. "All right. Shake?"

For a moment, everything seemed to freeze. Then D.G. laughed. He took Everett's hand and shook it vigorously. "We just don't know each other yet, right? And how are we supposed to be friends if we don't do something friends do, right?"

Everett grinned. That made sense. "So what's with these aliens?"

Beaming that smile, D.G. said, "Okay, first, we'll have to communicate with some special kind of language or something if we want to defeat them. So we'd better begin."

"Begin what?"

"Our special language," D.G. explained. "We only need a few words today. Since we're going into the trenches, we'll probably need something to tell which way to go. So when we mean 'go to the right' we say, '*Walla walla rye.*' When we mean 'go to the left' we say, '*Walla walla lee.*' When we want to go forward, it's '*Hoo coo for.*' And back . . ."

"Wait a minute," Everett interrupted. "If the aliens can hear us, they can hear us now talking about this, right?"

D.G. smiled. "Hey, you're no dummy, are you?"

Both of them laughed.

D.G. went on. "You're right. They can hear. But these aliens aren't that smart—right? They're the real dummies. I mean how smart can an alien be who dresses up in a baseball cap, overalls, and a greasy undershirt?"

Laughing, Everett got into the routine. "Okay, what's '*back*' again?"

" '*Hoo coo ack.*' "

"Got it. *Walla walla rye. Walla walla lee. Hoo coo for. Hoo coo ack.*"

"Excellent. *Hoo coo for,* soldier!"

They hustled around among the piles of trees and debris. When they were in sight of the school, D.G. pushed Everett's shoulder. "Get down!"

D.G.'s strength surprised Everett, and he stooped and

peered out at the school. Several men walked around doing construction work among the girders. "Shouldn't we have a special word for that?"

Squinting, D.G. nodded. "What do you say?"

Everett scratched his nose and watched the men a moment. "How about '*Grok mok*'?"

"Excellent. *Grok mok*, sergeant."

Everett waited.

"*Hoo coo for*," D.G. whispered and scurried forward bent low to the ground.

Everett followed him, staying behind tree branches and piled junk so as not to be seen. They darted around the fringes of the building on the south side near Everett's house. He noticed his brother Lance playing in the backyard, but he didn't say anything about it.

Suddenly, D.G. fell flat on the ground. "Hit the dirt, Sarge." He paused. "I mean *grok mok hok*. That means all the way down."

They both craned their necks from low on the ground and peered at the building. A man in overalls and a white undershirt with a red bandanna around his head was throwing pieces of wood into a fifty-gallon drum. He was well built, thick in the chest and belly. Everett could hear him mumbling as he fed the fire. Smoke billowed up out of the drum and blackened the air. The man coughed several times and talked to himself, then turned to go back in among the girders.

"The Jackal," whispered D.G.

"The Jackal?"

"One of the aliens. A particularly smelly one, I might add. He already yelled at me once about hanging around the building. Said I could get hurt. I should've dropped him with a round stone from my sling." D.G. smiled his crinkly smile.

"What should we do?" Everett's heart was pounding, and he felt excited and expectant.

"We have to get to the trenches without being seen. If they spot us, we're dead. They'll fry us in that incinerator and send our souls up in the smoke into their invisible ship. But first . . ."

He peered out at the building and shaded his eyes with his right hand. "Let's move in for a closer view."

Everett squinted his eyes and took a sharper look at the building. The Jackal was now out of sight. He wondered how they could get any closer without being spotted.

"See those girders there?" D.G. murmured and pointed. "We'll have to belly our way all the way to them."

"Right." Everett wasn't going to act afraid, even if he was a little.

"Okay, *grok mok hok* and let's go forward." D.G. paused as though thinking hard. "I mean *hoo coo for*." For a moment, he turned and looked at Everett, as though seeing into him. "Oh, doggie bones. I forgot. What is it?"

"*Hoo coo for*." Everett rolled his eyes. *Doggie bones*. That was a new one.

D.G. nodded. "Hey, you're not dumb." He gave him a

fierce look, then said, "We have to look tough, right?"

"Yeah. Bite The Jackal's toes off." Everett laughed. *D.G. is all right,* he thought. *He doesn't always order me around like Chuck used to.*

With a confident grin, D.G. dug in with his sneakers. "All right, let's go."

They both crawled on their elbows and bellies toward the pile of girders. It was hard going, and both of them were sweating in a few minutes. Every few feet, D.G. stopped and listened. Everett's heart thumped in his chest and he noticed his palms were wet. Dirt stuck to his fingers.

In five minutes they reached the girders. It was a pile about four feet high, white with concrete dust, and painted red. It gave them about six feet of cover as long as they ducked down. They both sat there panting, their backs against the dusty, cool metal. D.G. glanced at his watch. "Ten hundred fifteen hours, Sarge. We've got to find out more about this Jackal. Let me take a look."

D.G. crouched and looked through a space between the girders. Suddenly, D.G. whistled. "Alien k rations," he said and sat down. "We've got to check them out."

Everett looked at him, wondering what he meant.

"His lunch," whispered D.G. "What the aliens eat."

Rising, Everett peered through the girders, and saw the black lunch box at the far right edge. He was sure this was what D.G. referred to. They were going to take The Jackal's lunch? He felt his heart jolt and he wondered what The Jackal would do if he knew that. He sank down, then looked fearfully at D.G. He could tell the boy's mind was set. But deep down he liked it. Even if The Jackal came around, what could he do—curse at them? Call the cops, maybe?

"I'll have to sneak around and heist it," D.G. said. "It's simple. You keep a lookout. If any of the aliens look this way, let me know. Immediately. Got it?"

Everett nodded. His heart was drumming.

As D.G. crawled to the right edge of the girders, Everett stood and stared toward the team of men drinking coffee and joking far down at the other end of the building. D.G. stuck his head out, then disappeared out of sight on the right side of the girders. A second later, Everett saw D.G.'s hand whip up, grab the handle of the lunch box, and whisk it out of sight. Moments later, he was back behind the girders. Everett sank down.

D.G. had it opened before Everett could think through the consequences of what they were doing. "Now we'll see what aliens really eat."

There was a gray thermos bottle with a red cap, a sandwich, a small red apple, and a pack of Twinkies.

D.G. whistled. "I never would have thought aliens would be into Twinkies! This is far out."

Everett laughed, then covered his mouth and glanced back.

"So what should we do with them?" said D.G. "Should we have a bite, just to make sure it's the real thing?"

That was not a good idea, Everett thought. Taking The Jackal's lunch. But . . .

Before he could finish his thought, D.G. said, "No, we kill aliens. But we don't steal from them—right?" He peered at Everett and slit his eyes craftily. "No, we'll just leave this alien a little gift."

He pulled a felt pen out of his pocket. Looking around, he found a fist-sized stone, oblong, but flat on each side. "We'll send some shivers up The Jackal's spine, I'll tell you."

With a shrewd little grin, D.G. wrote on the stone: ALIENS—DIE! Then D.G. flipped it over. "What should we put on the back?"

Thinking quickly, Everett said, "How about, 'the Israelis'?"

D.G. chuckled. "You're not dumb!" He wrote in big letters: THE ISRAELIS. He plunked the rock into the lunch box next to the apple, then lay the sandwich on top of it. "This'll shiver his timbers."

Behind them, there was a sudden low grumble. "Now where is that little lunch box?" someone said with a phlegmy voice as if he had a cold.

Everett's neck prickled. D.G. froze and stared at Everett. They both sat very still, listening.

The voice said, "Hey, Sam. I thought you said you put my lunch box over here."

Another voice answered from down farther in the building. "I did, man. It's right there on the end."

They could hear whoever it was shuffling around in front of the girders. He mumbled under his breath about someone with the sense of two-penny nails. D.G. put the lunch box down very quietly. He motioned to Everett to get on his feet, slowly. They both rose soundlessly.

Everett's heart boomed. He readied himself and put his foot against a girder to give him a fast exit.

"He probably put it back here," the voice said.

They could hear his booted feet crunching on the concrete back toward them.

Everett steadied himself, and D.G held up his hand.

Suddenly, they both saw the edge of The Jackal's white shirt coming around the corner. D.G.'s hand flew down.

"*Walla walla for!*" he shouted.

Both of them sped out and ran across the yard back toward the tree piles. The Jackal's voice shouted out in surprise a moment later. "What the . . ."

They stopped behind a pile of trees and watched The Jackal quietly pick up the lunch box. He stood there holding his lunch box and going through it. Everett and D.G. watched as the big man pulled out the rock and looked at it. Then he laughed and threw it in their direction. "That's one for the book, boys!" he yelled. They both dropped down. The rock thudded about thirty feet away.

D.G. turned around. "He didn't seem too angry," he whispered.

Then he started to giggle. He turned to Everett. "That was great, wasn't it? You could tell The Jackal was upset, though. I think."

Everett was still gasping. He noticed he had to go to the bathroom. He didn't think The Jackal seemed very angry. But he said to D.G., "Excuse me. I've got to go!"

D.G. laughed. "You, too?"

A minute later, they hurried back to the trees and looked across at the school. The Jackal was out of sight. D.G. said, "I bet that guy eats onions and salami all day long. Imagine what his breath smells like."

Everett wrinkled his nose.

"Remember that commercial—the girl breathes on the guy and he disappears?"

Everett laughed. He'd always thought that one was particularly dumb.

"That was The Jackal's girl friend!" D.G. said. "And did you see how his belly button was hanging out!" D.G. said again. "I mean you could stick a watermelon in that thing. And it would stay."

They both erupted with laughter.

"I bet when The Jackal gets dirty enough he can grow tomato plants in it!"

Getting into the comic rhythm, Everett answered. "Maybe we should go back and check. My mom likes Jersey tomatoes."

D.G. laughed and looked at Everett gleefully. "I told you this would be great!"

Everett nodded and smiled. *Man, if Chuck had only seen that.* But he pushed the thought away. It didn't matter. They'd had some fun. That was what counted.

"So you want to go in the trenches?" D.G. said again.

Looking off to the other side of the school, Everett realized D.G. must be referring to the pipeline trenches they were digging there. "We'd better be careful," he said absently. "The Jackal'll be on the lookout."

D.G. nodded in agreement. "No problem. He's probably trying to figure out how to get that watermelon out of his belly button."

Grinning, Everett answered, "My dad knows a good doctor. Should we recommend him?"

"All right. Enough jokes," D.G. said, holding up his hand. "Let's go around in front of the houses and come in from the other side. You've got to use the surprise method. Like Entebbe Airport."

Everett didn't know what that was. But D.G. sprinted out toward the houses at the far end of the street before Everett could ask. "Come on," D.G. yelled. "We've got to stop those aliens! Today!"

Everett took a deep breath and sped after him.

7
The Frog

As they rounded the bend back toward the school, D.G. stopped and looked at one of the houses going up across the street from Everett's house.

"Wow!" D.G. said. "Look at that place!"

The house was ritzy, with a stone front—big white and gray glistening chunks of granite set in concrete—and the front door had pillars on either side of it. It was far bigger than Everett's house. They shuffled up to the front yard and stared at it for a few moments. Then after a quick glance around, Everett tiptoed up to a window and looked in. The house was empty.

"Pretty big rooms. Maybe they'll have a pool table or something useful like that in there." Everett realized D.G. had forgotten about the trenches and The Jackal. But he liked the idea of exploring at the moment more than having another meeting with the big man at the school.

They skulked around to the back. The moment they came around the corner, Everett let out a startled cry. In the backyard sat a white-aproned, rectangular swimming pool. It had no water in it yet, but the sides were eggshell white with a trim of marble around the edge.

"Hey, we've got to make friends with these folks," said D.G. with an admiring whistle. "I'm already sweating and that pool could prove to be a real cooler-offer." He smiled. "Maybe they'll be kids our age, and then we won't even need an invitation."

Everett sidled closer to the pool and looked down into it. It was about thirty or forty feet long, fifteen feet wide. The right end was shallow and it sloped down to the left into a drain. The drain must have been clogged up, because a foot or two of green, slimy-looking water stretched about ten feet across in the drainage hole.

D.G. said, "Let's climb down into it. We'd better check out that water. The Loch Ness monster might have taken up residence there. Or maybe even Flipper or someone. Maybe this is where The Jackal takes his baths."

"Hey, The Jackal's okay," Everett said absently.

D.G. nodded. "I know. I decided I like the guy too."

Scurrying to the shallow end of the pool, D.G. hopped

down. Everett followed. He noticed that their voices echoed in the pool once they were inside. The concrete was dusty with a white, creamy kind of dust. D.G. edged down the sloping floor of the pool to the dirty water around the drain.

"This stuff is gross," he said, stooping at the algae-coated water. "They'd better clean it up if they expect me to swim in it."

"You sound like you own the place already."

"Hey, they want D.G. around, they have to keep a clean act. That's all." He smiled and rubbed his hands on his jeans. "It kind of smells. Probably been here for a year. But there might be something in it." He threw in a stone.

Besides the stone, something else splashed.

"What was that?"

Everett watched the water. "Maybe it was a frog or something. Frogs like this kind of water."

D.G. threw in another stone. "He'd better come up and show himself if he knows what's good for him. The people who're gonna live here, you don't know what they might do to him. Especially if they have birds or cats. They might even be into frog legs."

As D.G. talked, Everett inspected the water. He knew the frog or whatever it was had to come up for air. Suddenly, he detected two eyes peering at him just over the surface of the water. "There he is," he yelled. "It's a frog. A big bull. Maybe we can catch him."

"Definitely," said D.G. and pivoted. "Where is he?"

Everett pointed. The frog didn't move, but its big green

eyes were fixed on both of the boys. "Maybe we can scare him out onto the concrete."

The frog was huge, a body maybe four or five inches long. The big bull head regarded them with round, light-green eyes and black pupils.

"What can we use?" said D.G., looking around.

Everett ran to the edge of the pool and pulled himself out. "I can beat him out with a stick. You try to catch him." He grabbed a broken branch from a nearby tree and rushed back. A moment later, he tried poking the frog with the stick. The frog dove but D.G. ran around to the other side of the pool. "Set up a commotion on that side. Let's see if he comes out over here."

Everett began beating the water with the stick. Sure enough, the frog popped up over on the side near D.G.

Then D.G. spotted a piece of screen lying in the back-yard. "This'll get that little greenie," he said, clasping it in his hand.

He rushed to the other side of the pool. Everett began beating the water, reaching out as far as he could. A moment later they forced the frog onto the screen, and D.G. flipped it out of the water. The big frog came down on its back. It rolled over and was ready to jump. But D.G. was quicker and brought his hands down on top of it.

Everett ran around to help him. "His skin feels gross."

D.G. laughed. "Yeah, I wouldn't want to take him in my room and put him in my bed for the night like you read in some books."

The frog pushed against their hands and tried to wriggle out. Everett shifted position. "What do you think we should do now?"

Suddenly, a strange voice spoke tartly above them, "You can start by getting out of our pool."

8
Linc and Tina

Everett froze, then twisted around to look up. The sides of the pool were far over his head at this point. But standing on the edge above him were two kids, a girl and a boy. They were both about the same size, and even looked alike. The girl had her hands on her hips and she appeared angry.

D.G. stood up. The moment he did, the frog wriggled away from Everett. He was free. D.G. made no effort to catch him. "Now look what happened."

The girl went on, "Who said you could play in *our* pool?"

D.G. suddenly threw up his hands. "Look, do you want

to help us catch *your* frog in *your* pool, or what? This is not the time to be asking questions. We can answer everything later. Meanwhile, you've got an alien invader in your pool."

Both of the kids gazed at him, amazed. Then the boy shrugged and looked at the girl. He said, "He's right, you know. That frog shouldn't be in the pool."

The boy ran down to the end of the pool. The girl then threw her hands up with a sigh and followed him. In a moment they stood with D.G. and Everett in the bottom of the pool.

The boy said, "What do we do?"

"We'll try to scare him out of the water again," said D.G.

"Okay, you—oh, we don't even know your names."

"We're twins," said the girl quickly. "My name is Christina Watterson. But everyone calls me Tina. This is Lincoln. He goes by Linc."

Both Tina and Linc had reddish blond, curly hair and a slash of freckles across their noses. They were wearing shorts and T-shirts.

D.G. said, "I'm D.G. and this is Everett. Everett lives across the street."

"Okay, everyone spread out," said D.G. "Everyone grab some stones and get ready." The frog was floating again in the middle of the pool, quiet and unblinking.

D.G. passed out extra stones to Linc and Tina and gave everyone instructions. He submerged the screen near the frog.

Tina, Linc, and Everett stirred the water and splashed. The frog dove several times, but in two minutes they had the frog on the screen and threw him out of the water. Linc snatched it and held it up.

"Pretty, isn't he?" he said. The frog twisted and squirmed in his fingers.

D.G. laughed. "Hey, you're good with those hands."

Turning to Tina, Linc said, "You want to hold him?"

Tina made a face, then shook her head. "I'll just touch him." She gingerly poked his head and the frog shot its mouth open. Tina leaped back.

"He doesn't have any teeth," Linc said, and advanced toward her. Tina jumped out of the way and ran to the edge of the pool. "You're not putting him in my face," she cried.

Linc ran after her. D.G. and Everett began laughing, but Tina gave them a hard look, and they stopped.

"Come on," D.G. said, "Let's put the frog somewhere where he can't get away."

"I have the perfect thing," said Linc. "Here, you take the frog for a minute," he said, holding it out to Everett.

The frog felt squishy and slimy in his hands. Linc climbed out of the pool and disappeared into the garage. Tina said, "So what do we call him?"

D.G. looked at Everett. "How about Goliath?" he said. "Except we won't kill him and cut his head off."

Tina laughed. "Great. This is fun."

Linc returned with a huge pickle jar. "It was left in the garage by the workmen, I guess," he explained. "We can punch holes in the top, and the frog'll be fine." He looked at Tina. "I told Dad we were out back for a while. He said it was okay. But he wants us to come in at twelve. We're going to get something to eat up on the highway."

"Okay," Tina answered, and looked back at D.G. and Everett.

Linc dropped Goliath into the jar and turned the lid. "I'll put some holes in it."

But D.G. shook his head. "I think we ought to let him go. We can take him down to Rocky Creek."

Tina and Linc looked at Everett, then back at D.G.

With a sudden, eager grin, Linc said, "You mean you don't want me to hide him in the foot of Tina's bed tonight?"

Giving Linc a shove, Tina wrinkled her face. "Yuck!" But everyone else laughed. A moment later, Tina laughed. "That's okay," she said. "I'll just sneak him into your room and stuff a leg into your ear. How would you like that?" She stuck out her tongue at Linc and everyone laughed again.

Nodding with excitement, D.G. said, "This way he won't get sucked up in the drain or something. You're going to be cleaning this up and putting swimming water in it, right?"

"Yeah, and we can all swim," Tina answered. "You're all invited."

"Well, let's get Goliath into the creek," D.G. concluded, "Unless . . . "

Everett looked at him and waited. He was used to these sudden silences now.

"Unless what?" Linc said.

"Unless someone wants to put him between two matzos and have him for lunch." D.G. gazed around at everyone as though waiting for a laugh.

Tina held her nose. "That's gross."

Linc looked at him in the jar. "I think we'll let some fish have him."

They all walked lazily toward the creek at the base of the yard, talking and laughing. Then D.G. suddenly galloped on ahead and raced along the edge, looking for a place to let the frog go. "Over here," he called to the other three.

Linc opened the jar and laid it on the bank. Goliath immediately hopped out and dove into the water. They watched him kick under the surface, a perfect breaststroke. With a splash out onto the bank, he disappeared among the shrubbery on the other side of the creek.

Suddenly, D.G. shouted. He had run up the creek about thirty yards and was standing under a tree. "This is perfect," he called. "I can't believe how lucky we are."

Everyone ran over to the tree. Its branches hung way out over Rocky Creek. It was thick, about three feet in diameter. An oak, Everett thought. It would be easy to climb.

"We can hang the rope up there," D.G. said, pointing to a branch hanging far out over the creek.

Everett stared at D.G. "What do you mean?"

"For the rope swing over to the other side," D.G. said.

"That way we can establish a permanent beachhead to move in our provisions. So we can explore the forest. Who knows what we'll find?"

Tina stepped up to the tree and ran her hand across the trunk. She looked at D.G. and Everett a little amazed.

Everett suddenly had an idea. "I can climb up and tie the rope."

D.G. nodded. "That'll be perfect. All we need is a rope." D.G. looked up at the tree. Linc said that they had one from a rope and tire swing they'd had at their previous home. But Everett noticed both Linc and Tina looking at D.G.'s birthmark.

"That's his birthmark," Everett suddenly said, hoping it wouldn't matter.

Tina smiled. "I thought so. Linc and I both have one in the same place. Right in the middle of our backs above our behinds. Do you want to see?"

D.G. laughed. "No, that's okay. We'll pass on that one. We'll call you 'Scarbutts.' "

Then he looked at his watch. "Almost twelve hundred hours. I think some of us have to get some k rations. The rest of us have to head home. But what about that rope? You'll bring it tomorrow?" He gazed expectantly at Tina and Linc with that happy, sparkling light in his eyes.

Immediately, Tina's eyes fell. "Oh, drat. We won't be back for a week after this. We're staying at our grandmother's until everything's moved in over the weekend."

Shrugging, D.G. looked around at everyone. His curly

hair seemed to point every which way. Everett noticed that his eyebrows almost grew together. "Well, then, we'll look for you in a week," D.G. said, not appearing disappointed.

"Guess we better go," Linc said. "But we're glad we met you."

Everett caught Tina regarding him with a warm smile and felt embarrassed. But he liked the way that D.G. took over as leader. It made him feel good. D.G. was the kind of leader who included everyone and didn't act all high and mighty about it.

Like Chuck.

Yeah, Everett thought, stealing another look at Tina. He began to feel that things were really going well, and he enjoyed it. He already liked Linc and Tina and suddenly he hoped that they'd be good friends, people he could count on.

D.G. suddenly dashed up the hill, but just before he reached the top, he turned and yelled, "One week!" then cried to Everett, "See you later, crocodile!" He disappeared around the far edge of the house. Tina and Linc laughed as they all walked slowly up the hill with Everett.

"Does he always talk like that?" Tina asked, walking next to Everett.

"Only when he talks," Everett answered. They all chuckled.

They reached the house and Tina introduced Everett to her parents. They were both tall and slim, and Mrs. Watterson was almost as pretty as his own mother. They invited him to come swimming when they had the pool ready.

Then Everett left for home. He thought maybe he'd come back over that afternoon. As he ran into the house, he called, "I'm hungry, Mom! What's for lunch?"

9
Trenches

Two days later, D.G. and Everett did more exploring on the street the school was on. D.G. remembered the trenches in front of it.

Though Everett's street was paved with asphalt, this one wasn't paved at all. It was flat, tan dirt and sand, being prepared for the macadam. Everett hadn't done much searching around it the last few weeks because of the construction. Along the left edge of the street, though, strung a long ditch with huge concrete pipes joined together.

"Drainage pipes," said D.G. and gave a low whistle. He

turned to Everett. "This might lead right up the aliens' front door."

Everett was worried again about bumping into Chuck and Stuart. Chuck's house sat right at the end of the street. He glanced around, his heart beginning to thump as he glanced at the big house. "Just don't let them show up," he prayed, then felt guilty inside about thinking such a thing.

D.G. turned around and spotted an open concrete drain. He grabbed Everett's arm and said, "All we have to do is climb down and we're in. Who knows where it comes out?"

"What if it comes out right under their noses?"

"Then we'll blast them off their faces!" said D.G. with a snort. "We aren't afraid of The Jackal. He's just a tub of sausage."

Everett peered around nervously as D.G. climbed over the edge of the drain. "It's open," D.G. said. "We can go down into it."

A metal ladder was built in along the side of the drain and they both climbed down about eight feet into the pit. The pipe veered off in three directions, one toward the school and the others up and down Everett's street. The odor of stale water hung in the air.

Water lines stained the bottom of the pipes with scraggly edges of red and brown. Cool air drifted into Everett's face, much cooler than the air outside. He closed his eyes and enjoyed the refreshing touch.

"I think we should go up this way," said D.G., pointing

toward the school. "We may not be able to get out the other ways." His voice echoed in the chamber, making an eerie sound. "You will come, won't you?"

Everett sucked in one last breath of fresh air and nodded. He wasn't going to let D.G. think he was afraid. Their feet made echoing swishing noises as they scraped along. They straddled the water and stepped into a narrowing darkness.

Then, just as Everett thought there was no end, they heard noises and saw light shimmering down from above about thirty feet ahead.

"Another drain," said D.G.

He hurried forward. Everett was right on his heels. When they reached the drain, they heard a man's voice.

"Let's break for coffee, Charley. It's hotter than a cat in a tin box, too hot for this kind of work."

They heard a man's boots crunching on the dirt. Moments later, the sound was gone.

"That sounded like The Jackal," whispered D.G.

He edged cautiously out into the square concrete area of the drain and looked up, shielding his eyes with his hand from the sun. It had the same kind of ladder as the other one.

"I'd better take a look," said D.G., not giving Everett a chance to answer. He climbed the ladder and peered out. Then he turned and whispered to Everett. "We're about thirty yards from the school. Right in front of it. Come on up."

Everett climbed up the ladder next to D.G. and listened when he got to the edge. Then he stuck his head out.

As D.G. swiveled, he suddenly yelped, "Hey, would you look at that?"

Twisting, Everett immediately saw a yellow bulldozer and a power shovel standing idle about two yards from the drain. The men obviously had been shoveling dirt over the pipe.

"We'll have to sabotage their machines," said D.G. "Terminate all routes of escape."

He looked at Everett with slit eyes. "You ready for action?"

Everett gulped and looked beyond the dozer nervously. Instantly, he saw Chuck and Stuart walking casually up the street toward the bulldozer.

The moment he saw them, Everett shrank down. He couldn't let them see him. But in the same instant, a plan flashed into Everett's mind. No, maybe this was his big chance. This might show them he was no coward.

"I wonder if the key is in it," Everett said, glancing from the bulldozer to D.G. to Chuck and Stuart and back again.

D.G. stared at him with wide eyes. "You wouldn't try to start it, would you?"

Giving D.G. a let-me-show-you-what-life's-all-about-kid look he'd seen Chuck make a million times, he said, "I'll show you."

Grabbing Everett's arm, D.G. looked deeply into his eyes. "That's pretty dangerous."

"No problem," Everett said. "All we do is look. Come on."

Everett pulled himself out of the concrete hole and darted around behind the bulldozer. D.G. kept behind him. Crouching down, Everett checked the men sitting at the school. They were talking and laughing. No one seemed to notice them.

Glancing at D.G., Everett looked down the street for Chuck or Stuart, then smiled and climbed onto the bulldozer. Over his shoulder, he noticed that both boys stopped, watching the scene. A moment later, Everett bounced onto the seat and looked for a key.

Out of the corner of his eye, Everett watched the building. The Jackal and his friends made no move in their direction. Then he saw the key.

D.G. stood on the ground by the treads, still bobbing to keep out of sight. "Are you sure you should start it?" Everett could tell he was very nervous.

"Let's just see what happens." He turned the key. Instantly, the bulldozer motor turned over. A moment later, the engine roared and black smoke shot up out of the stack. The roar was so loud, it almost made him fall off the tractor. As his arm flailed for a hold, he hit a control and the front shovel began to come up. "Oh, no!"

D.G.'s face was white, except for his birthmark, which seemed almost to glow. Everett panicked, not knowing what to do to stop the shovel.

He whipped around to see if anyone from the building

was looking. The Jackal and the men had all turned and were staring in their direction.

"Get down, Everett, they see us," D.G. yelled. Everett jumped off the tractor. He noticed Chuck and Stuart both laughing and pointing at him.

"Let's run for it." D.G. shrieked.

The shovel jolted higher and Everett turned in time to see the men shout, "Hey, you kids!" All four of them jumped up and lunged for the boys.

Everett ran around to the other side of the bulldozer. D.G. seemed frozen in place, gaping in terror. The Jackal ran toward them with the others. His eyes looked wide with fright, or was it anger? They were only about twenty yards away now. Two of the other men shouted and cursed at them.

Everett yelled to D.G., "Let's run!" then bolted around the front of the dozer and sprinted toward the north end of the school. D.G. hopped into the farther trench on the other side of the drain and hurried down it, like a crazy man on a tightrope.

Immediately, Everett knew D.G. couldn't get away. One of the men got ahead of D.G. and jumped into the trench. He was big, tall, and lean. He had a beard and a dark, scowling face. He cursed as he jumped into the trench and pivoted, his face flushed, and twisted with rage. He had a belt in his hand. He swore at D.G., saying he would give him a spanking he wouldn't forget.

Everett stopped and turned around, desperate to do something fast. He knew he couldn't let D.G. get caught. It wasn't even D.G.'s fault. But The Jackal and another man were about fifteen yards behind D.G. on the equipment, turning it off.

D.G. was trapped. The small boy stopped and stared at the big man with the beard. The man spread his arms and said to him, "Come to papa, punk." Fear turning into panic, Everett picked up a dirt bomb and shouted at the big man. "Let him go." The Jackal and the other man stopped the bulldozer.

The big man glanced back at Everett and laughed. "You don't scare me, kid."

He advanced on D.G. and the smaller boy backed up. Everett took a breath, then hurled the dirt clod. It struck the trench right behind the big man.

The man turned and swore. "If you know what's good for you, punk, you better not do that!"

He spun and looked back at D.G. "A bird in hand is better than two in the bush." He had a cocky grin on his face and rumbled forward.

Breathing fast, Everett grabbed another clod of dirt. His only chance was to hit the man in the behind. He slung it sidearm at the big man. The clod was true. It struck him in the center of his overalls on his behind. The man swore. He wheeled around. "I'm gonna get you now, punk. No more messing around."

Everett shouted at D.G. to get out of the trench and run.

D.G. gave him a terrified look, but Everett reversed

direction to run. The moment he did, his foot caught in a hole and he fell. His ankle twisted. As he tried to get up, it didn't hold. He fell again and a moment later, the big man lifted him, helpless, by the belt.

"I'm going to give you a good tannin', punk!"

Everett wriggled around in time to see D.G. leap on the man's back and hit him with his fists. "Let him go! Let him go!"

The man dropped Everett and pinned him with one arm, then twisted to shake D.G. off. Moments later, The Jackal and the other two men arrived, puffing and wheezing, and pulled D.G. off the big man's back, holding him in place. D.G. tried to wrestle away, but The Jackal's arms were strong and hard.

The big man let Everett get up. "Stand up, kid, you're in big trouble."

One of the other men said, "We ought to call the police on you two. Starting a bulldozer! You could have been killed."

Everett, paralyzed with fear, glanced at D.G. helplessly, then hung his head.

"And messin' with my lunch," The Jackal said, a slight smile crossing his grizzled face.

Everett tried to think of something to say. If they called the cops, his father would hit the roof. Then he saw Chuck and Stuart still standing beyond them, gaping at the whole scene.

The big man gripped Everett's arm. "You can't go

messing around with that kind of equipment," he said, and swore at Everett. He looked from Everett to D.G., then added, pointing at Everett, "This one was the one on the tractor and who hit me with the dirt ball. We can let this other one go."

For a moment, D.G. looked terrified. Then his face set with resolve. The Jackal hesitated, then let go of D.G. "Okay, you can go now, son."

Swallowing, Everett tried to think of what to say. He was done for. His parents would kill him. He began, "It *was* my fault—"

But suddenly, D.G. answered fiercely, "I'm not going. I'm just as responsible as Everett. Whatever you do to him, you do to me."

Everett stared at D.G., surprised and amazed. D.G. had his chin set and his birthmark blazed.

The man snorted, and The Jackal hesitated again, then smiled. "All right. You're going to be loyal to your friend, huh? Like David and Jonathan?"

D.G. nodded, his eyes suddenly growing wide with interest.

"I say we give both of them a good whipping," said the big man, fingering his belt.

Everett gulped, but The Jackal said, "That's illegal. Anyway, kids, if you promise you won't mess around here anymore, we'll just let you go."

"Boss!" said the big man.

The Jackal waved him off. "We don't have time for

this." He turned back to D.G. and Everett, bending down slightly. He had soft-looking brown eyes that glinted with a friendly light. "What do you say, boys? You're not going to play around here anymore, right? At least not on the equipment and not with people's lunches—right?"

The air seemed to hang suspended with the heat and the silence. Then D.G. looked up at Everett, waiting. Everett blinked. He couldn't believe they were just going to let them go. But he nodded and rubbed his toe in the dirt. "I'm sorry. I shouldn't have gotten on that tractor. Or hit you with the dirt bomb. I'm sorry."

The big man shook his head, but The Jackal smiled and held out his hand. "All right. We were kids once, too."

Everett looked up into The Jackal's eyes. "Thanks, sir."

The Jackal said, with a twinkle in his eye, "Just remember, though, we aren't aliens! Just little old construction workers."

D.G. smiled at him, glanced at the other men, and said, "Thanks!" He started to walk back toward the houses, giving the men a wave. Everett staggered after him, his ankle hurting beneath him. Chuck and Stuart watched them as they walked along, and suddenly Chuck called out, "Hey, Abels, good show!"

Everett tried to pretend he hadn't heard, but D.G. stopped. "Isn't that Chuck Davis?"

"We thought you were just a yellow belly," Chuck yelled again, "but we were wrong, Abels. Now we know you're also a jerk."

He slapped Stuart on the back, and they turned to go, still laughing. Everett hunched his shoulders, feeling cut down and foolish. He wished he could disappear into the ground. But D.G. led him back to the mounds. When they stopped to look back at the school, D.G. peered at Everett. "What were you trying to do, give me a heart attack?"

Everett said, "I'm sorry. I really am. I shouldn't have done that." He walked fretfully to the front of the tank, and stood there panting. He felt miserable and more hopeless than ever, but then he thought of how D.G. had stood up for him. "How come you did that?"

"What?"

"They would have let you go."

Instantly, D.G. looked down at his feet, looking uncomfortable. "I don't know. I just felt it was right."

Everett swallowed. D.G. was something, that was for sure. He nodded. "Thanks. You didn't have to do that."

"It's okay. It was nothing. I wanted to. You helped me too, though."

Everett remembered throwing the dirt bomb. "Yeah, well . . ."

"Well, that proves it."

"Proves what?"

"We're really friends."

With a lump hardening in his throat, Everett looked back where Chuck and Stuart had been. He thought again about how he'd run from O'Brien when Chuck and Stuart fought him. Maybe he really wasn't a coward.

He suddenly noticed D.G. smiling his crinkly smile.
"That Jackal's all right. Maybe his belly button isn't so big
after all."

Sitting down with a weary sigh, Everett remembered
how once Chuck and Stuart had turned against him in a
baseball card flip, accusing him of cheating in front of some
others. He hadn't been cheating, and he'd wondered why
they did it. It was one of those times when they'd had a
"falling out," as he called it. He wondered if D.G. ever
turned against people like that. He tried to watch D.G.'s
face out of the side of his eyes. He was such a happy person.
Even with all he took at school, he seemed happy. What
was it about him?

He thought miserably again of Chuck's words. "You're
just a jerk!" Then he remembered D.G.'s face as he refused
to be freed by the construction workers. "You're really
something, D.G."

D.G. ran his fingers along the log as though in deep
thought. Then he said, "Well, let's get into the tank and
wipe out some imaginary Arabs. We need something a little
tamer."

They both climbed aboard the tank. After another half
hour or so, D.G. looked at his watch and whistled. "Oh,
boy, I'm late. My mom'll kill me. I've got to go. See you
tomorrow or maybe even later on this afternoon?" He
looked hopefully at Everett.

This time Everett didn't hesitate. "Sure, but where do
you have to go?"

"My mom makes me study in the early afternoon. I didn't do so well in school this past year." He looked down at his feet and shifted his weight, then glanced back up with that crinkly smile. "I almost had to go to summer school."

Everett watched D.G.'s dark eyes. He wondered why he was always so honest. He knew Chuck and Stuart lied all the time about things. He knew he'd lied about things. But D.G. was like—he didn't hide anything. Wasn't he ever ashamed of anything?

Before Everett thought about it, he said, "Well, if you ever want me to help you out . . ."

D.G. grinned. "Thanks. I'll remember." As he walked away, he suddenly turned and said, "See you in the afternoon?"

"Of course."

"Maybe you can come over to my house," D.G. said. "We can play in my room or something." He pointed to the house on the opposite side of the school. "That one." Everett nodded. As he walked home, he thought about D.G. again. He was a good guy. Why did other kids reject him? It didn't make sense. He stuck with you. And his birthmark, that didn't really bother him. He was no dummy. In fact, he seemed smarter than a lot of kids, even Chuck. And Linc and Tina liked him.

So why did kids *dislike* him?

He couldn't figure it out. But one thing he knew, whatever happened, he wasn't just going to walk away now.

He realized D.G and he were friends. And soon Linc and Tina would be part of the group on a regular basis too. No way would he desert D.G. now.

Everett went over to D.G.'s house that afternoon and they made a fort in his basement. The Frankl cellar was a jumble of stored things, but it was fun building little niches with the furniture and drop cloths that covered them.

D.G.'s mother was a heavy woman with dark hair, a wide smile and bright eyes. She gave them some Tastykakes and milk in the late afternoon, adding, "I hope it doesn't ruin your dinner." Everett told her it wouldn't.

Then D.G. took him up to his room and showed him his model collection—planes, tanks, trucks—all carefully painted and laid out on his shelves. D.G. was a good painter; Everett could see that. Better than he or Chuck or Stuart had ever been.

As D.G. showed off his models, Everett noticed one shelf with about ten black-and-white speckled notebooks like they used in school, and he wondered what they were for. He figured it must have something to do with his studying, and he didn't ask D.G. about it. But somewhere in his memory he remembered there was something about D.G. and a notebook once. He couldn't remember what it was. D.G. always had a reputation as a strange kid. As Everett walked home that afternoon, he felt better about everything with D.G. He figured they could play together and be friends for sure now, regardless of what he had to do to get back in with Chuck. He told himself he wouldn't just drop D.G. He'd continue to be friends. Maybe he could even get Chuck and Stuart to like D.G. too. He was no wimp and he was fun. *Why not?* he thought. *D.G.'s all right.*

That night Everett overheard his mother say to his father, "Everett seems to be doing real well, Tom."

His father answered, "We'll see. I'm just glad he's found this new friend. What's his name?"

"D.G."

"What's that stand for?"

She laughed. "Strange name. From the Bible, Everett said. But he likes to go by his initials. Evvie said he didn't do very well in school last year, and that he has this birthmark on his face."

"I just hope things continue to go well."

"They will."

Everett liked to listen to his parents talk quietly at night. It gave him a feeling of peace, like all was well. He didn't know why. He just liked it.

10
The Slingshot

The next morning after breakfast, Everett gazed out toward the piles of trees behind the school. He still wondered if he should become fast friends with D.G. Would he ever get back in with Chuck and Stuart?

Still, something deep down wanted to. D.G. was fun. Everett could easily say that much. You never knew what to expect with him. And D.G. was honest, too. He didn't pretend. Everett decided again that meeting D.G. was good, and he didn't hesitate as he ran out to the tank.

They played in the tank all week, waiting for Linc and Tina to come back so they could get on with the rope swing. They made other explorations around the area, but nothing as exciting happened as "The Bulldozer Caper," as D.G. now called it.

On Thursday, D.G. and Everett followed Rocky Creek all the way up to the public swimming pool that many of the families in the neighborhood belonged to. Everett's mother took his brother and sister there a lot, but Everett hadn't gone swimming much this summer. He knew Chuck would be there.

When D.G. heard the noises of children yelling and playing, he wanted to see what it was, and Everett told him it was the pool. They walked through the woods to the fence around it, just beyond the diving area.

"Cool!" said D.G. "I wish my dad would let me join this place."

"You don't belong?"

"No. My dad and mom aren't interested. They say I can just use the sprinkler." D.G. raised his eyebrows and laughed. "They're not beach people, if you know what I mean."

A group of boys were running and diving off the low board and the high board. Everett thought about how he and Chuck and others had done that so many times last summer. They played games like Sharks and Minnows, raced the length of the pool, worked at flips and one-and-a-halfs off the low board, and did cannonballs and can openers to see who made the biggest splash.

"Well, let's go," Everett said.

D.G. didn't move. "Hey, look at this guy!"

Everett turned around and saw Moose Horgan jump off the high board and crash a huge cannonball into the pool. Everyone cheered and Moose climbed out, making muscles and laughing.

D.G. smiled. "It is cool."

"Yeah," said Everett and turned to walk back down the path. "Let's just go home."

They shuffled down the path. D.G. pulled at leaves and tree branches. He kept up a running monologue about swimming and guns and Israelis. Everett fought an inner battle of anger at Chuck and aggravation at D.G.'s good mood. D.G. suddenly said, "You used to be real close friends with that guy, Chuck Davis, didn't you?"

Swallowing back his surprise, Everett nodded morosely. "Yeah, for a while."

"How come you're not anymore?"

Not knowing what to answer, Everett decided not to bring up the O'Brien episode. "We just had a problem."

"How come he called you 'yellow belly'? I don't think you're a yellow belly."

Suddenly, Everett wheeled around. He wished D.G would just shut up sometimes. Why did he have to talk so much? The bitterness burst inside him, and he wanted to scream into D.G.'s face to stuff it! But when he saw D.G.'s sympathetic eyes, he couldn't be angry. He turned back around. "I just blew it, that's all."

D.G. was quiet, then said, "You don't have to tell me about it. I understand."

They walked along silently down the trail. A rabbit hopped across the path and squirrels skittered among the trees. Everett fidgeted, trying to force D.G.'s words out of his mind. He knew D.G. wouldn't put him down. He wasn't that kind of guy. But . . . Then a moment later, Everett turned and decided to tell D.G. about the fight with O'Brien.

When he was done, D.G. said, "Yeah, he's a nasty guy. He's picked on me, too." D.G. seemed to be thinking. They had stopped in a clearing by the creek. "But if you thought Chuck had given you the signal, it wasn't like you really were so afraid you'd desert them, right? You just thought Chuck gave the signal, right? So he should be willing to be friends again, right?"

"Tell him that." Everett felt better the way D.G. was talking. But he added, "I was afraid, though."

"Well, of course!" D.G. said with a roll of his eyes. "Who wouldn't be? O'Brien's like—Mister Kill-Everyone-the-Moment-They-Look-at-You-Wrong."

Everett laughed and D.G. raised his eyebrows with his triumphant look. Then Everett shifted his feet. "Yeah, well, it's over now. Chuck'll never be friends with me again."

Shifting his weight nervously, D.G. said, "Well, anyway, I'm kind of glad."

"Glad?"

"Well, if you were friends with him, maybe you and I wouldn't be friends like we are now, right?"

Staring at D.G. a moment, all of Everett's pain seemed

to swell and then evaporate. He smiled. "Yeah, maybe you're right."

They headed toward the bridge that went over Rocky Creek above the street where Everett lived. He wasn't sure whether to feel unhappy, angry, or relieved, but the lump in his throat kept growing. He realized now whatever happened he would never abandon D.G. No matter what Chuck said or did. D.G. was just too good a guy.

The next day, Everett and D.G. watched as bulldozers and steam shovels tore through the tree piles, including their tank, and loaded them onto dump trucks. In a few days the whole field would be clear, and they'd have no place to build or play.

D.G. turned soberly to Everett and said, "Well, there goes the tank. The Israelis lose one more time."

Everett wished Linc and Tina would hurry up and move in. A number of small moving trucks had been by during the week, but they hadn't seen the twins. It had never occurred to Everett that the trees would be cleared away one day, let alone so soon. What would they do now? He wanted to drag the workmen out of their machines and throttle them, even though The Jackal had waved to them twice as they watched.

Still, D.G. didn't seem in the least hurt or deterred. "It doesn't matter anyway," he said. "We've got much bigger plans than that old tank."

We do? Everett thought. He smiled to himself expectantly.

Did D.G. always think about a million miles ahead of everyone else?

D.G. turned around and surveyed their street. "We need to get ready for when Linc and Tina are back."

As D.G. stood looking down the road, Everett suddenly noticed the sling dangling from D.G.'s rear right pocket. He said, "So when are you going to teach me how to use that slingshot?"

"Oh, you want to?"

"Sure."

"All right. I'll teach you my best moves."

D.G. shook the thongs out and placed both ends in his hand, with the pouch dangling at the bottom, just touching the edge of his cutoff jeans. "Okay, this is how you do it. You put the stone in the pouch like this. Or a dirt bomb. Or whatever. A round stone is best." He knelt and found a pebble, then laid it in the pouch. It was more like a flat, leather patch with a small valley in the middle to hold the stone firmly. "The thing you have to learn is when to release it. You have to learn to think like an Israeli."

He squinted across the street. "Now see that telephone pole there?" He gestured toward one of the poles lying by the street ready to be pounded into the ground. "Let's see if I can hit it. Stand back."

He whirled the sling around his head, whipping it faster and faster. Suddenly, with a great "Yaaaaaa!" he let it go. The stone struck the pole in less than a second and bounced off toward a driveway. D.G. smiled. "Okay, you ready, Sarge?" Everett cautiously accepted the thong D.G. held out to him. He figured it couldn't be too difficult. D.G. wasn't exactly sportsman of the year.

"Remember," D.G. warned, "you have to feel for when it releases. It's all in your feel. It has to come naturally. You can't be told when to let go. You just practice and eventually it starts to feel right. Gradually you'll learn to think like a real Israeli."

Everett nodded and smiled to himself. It killed him the way D.G. was always talking about Israelis. He bent down to pick up a stone.

"Use a dirt bomb," D.G. said.

Everett knelt down and looked up at him. "Why?"

"It'll leave a solid mark. You'll know exactly where it hit. Then you can gauge it better for the next try."

Snorting with amusement, Everett picked up a small, brown hunk of dirt. It was sandy, but solid. It would crumble easily when it struck something. *So what should I shoot at?* he wondered. He decided he'd try for the telephone pole, too. But he didn't want to look like an idiot. If he missed, it wouldn't look good. But then, he told himself, D.G. wouldn't care. *He doesn't put you down for stuff like that.*

He slowly whirled the sling around his head. But it was too slow and the dirt bomb fell out.

"You have to get it going fast or it will fall out." D.G. said and backed up. "Just don't fire it at me."

Finding another dirt bomb, Everett laid it in the leather

pouch and swung the sling again. A moment later, it shot out behind him before he could even begin to aim.

"What am I doing wrong?" he said to D.G.

"Just get used to it. Make sure the projectile is in the pouch and swing it gently but quickly. It'll stay once you get used to the feel of it."

Projectile! Chuckling to himself, Everett tried two more dirt bombs before he got one to stay through several swings. But after the fourth one he managed to whip it forward, though still far to the left of the telephone pole.

"Fantastic!" D.G. yelled. "You're doing better than me when I first tried."

Everett snorted and looked at him. "Come on. That's pitiful."

With a little shrug, D.G. cocked his head sheepishly. "I have to lie about something, don't I?"

Everett laughed.

"No, really, I had a hard time with it. I know it's not easy. Now try it again."

Six clods of dirt later, Everett hit the telephone pole about five feet from where he was aiming.

D.G. shouted, "Yo!" then said, "Okay, you've got the range and the vertical right. Now you've got to get it on the mark horizontally."

This time Everett laughed out loud. Did D.G. always have to sound so technical? Shaking his head, Everett quickly fired another dirt bomb at the pole. It pinged off even closer to the mark.

After several more tries, they started up the street again, and Everett handed him the sling. D.G. waved his hand at him. "You keep it." He reached in his pocket and pulled out another one that Everett hadn't seen. "Isn't that what the Boy Scouts say—'Be prepared'? Well, I'm prepared. And I'm not even a Boy Scout."

Awed, Everett looked down at the sling. "Thanks. I didn't expect you to give me that one. I just thought you'd show me how to make one."

"Friends means you'd die for one another—right? So what's a slingshot?" said D.G. "Even if it is my best one." He raised his eyebrows. His deep-set eyes had that delighted, "the joke's on me" look that Everett was beginning to anticipate.

Then D.G. laughed. "Okay, so it's not the greatest one on earth. My dad has the greatest one. But it's broken in perfectly. So take it."

D.G. turned up the street to walk toward the house. After stuffing the sling into his pocket, Everett looked up and saw Chuck and Stuart strutting toward them.

"Oh, boy," Everett said, glancing at D.G.

Stopping, D.G. looked uneasily at Everett.

Chuck's hard-edged voice rang out. "Well, if it isn't the little yellow belly with Scarface."

11
Revelation

D.G. stopped abruptly and looked at Everett warily, then watched the two boys walk up to them. Chuck wore blue jean shorts and a blue T-shirt. Stuart had on a surfer swimsuit and shirt.

"So I see you guys have your weapons ready." Chuck gave D.G.'s slingshot a flick.

Everett's breath came in little spurts. *Why did this have to happen?*

"And I suppose you and Scarface are great friends now?"

Everett tightened up. Even if D.G. wasn't the coolest kid in school, he didn't like the way Chuck was talking. "His name is D.G."

Looking from Chuck to Everett, D.G. seemed nervous and kept shifting his weight. Suddenly, Chuck turned to D.G. "So did the yellow belly tell you how he deserted me and Stu here in the heat of battle with John O'Brien?"

D.G. slit his eyes and set his jaw. "He told me all about it."

Swallowing back his anger, Everett waited. D.G. didn't flinch. He simply stared down Chuck without saying anything else. Chuck was obviously deflated.

"Oh, so I guess it doesn't bother you at all?"

Not missing a beat, D.G. said, "I go by what I see, not by what I hear."

"Yeah, and what did you see?"

The heat of the morning seemed to press down on everyone. Suddenly Everett wished he could crawl into a crack in the telephone pole. "I've seen enough to know he's not a coward," D.G. said.

"Like what?"

"Like sticking with me in a bad situation."

Chuck seemed surprised. D.G. told him about The Jackal.

"Oh, yeah, we saw that."

For once Chuck seemed like the old Chuck, even friendly. "Yeah, well, it takes a lot more than turning on a bulldozer." He thumbed in Stuart's direction, trying to act tough again. "Come on, Stu. Let's leave these rejects to themselves."

Still fighting an urge to punch someone, Everett watched them go, laughing and talking between themselves, turning every now and then to look back. D.G. clenched and unclenched his fist. Everett's heart was drumming so loudly, he thought it would explode.

Then with a nasty smirk on his face, Chuck whipped around. "Still writing in your diary, Scarface?"

D.G.'s face went white. He shouted, "You just forget about my diary, Davis. Forget about it."

The moment he said it, Everett remembered. In fourth grade the three classes got together to show unique things each student had done. D.G. brought in his diary. He told everyone he kept it since the beginning of third grade. Chuck stole one of the books when D.G. wasn't looking and took it to a corner to read to some of the other kids. D.G. went berserk. He began screaming and running after Chuck like a maniac. The teacher broke it up and made Chuck apologize, but Chuck said afterward to Everett and Stuart, "I'd give anything to see what that moron puts in his diary."

As the realization burned into Everett's mind, Chuck shouted to D.G, "Yeah, well write a few lines about me! I'd like to see my name in print when it gets published!" He slapped Stuart on the back, then walked off down the road.

Yeah, still the same old Chuck, Everett thought bitterly. He studied D.G. and then Chuck. *That was what I saw in his room. Those black-and-white speckled notebooks.*

He wondered what D.G. might have written in them. But he immediately decided that was D.G.'s business. For the first time, he felt a real pride that D.G. was his friend.

D.G. was different, yes, but even if other kids didn't like him, maybe it was because they didn't know him. Chuck was being nasty for no reason. It was a side of him that Everett had never understood.

For a moment, Everett wondered why he'd ever been such good friends with Chuck. There were plenty of kids in fifth grade who disliked him. Why hadn't he seen it before?

D.G. wheeled around, his lips curled in anger. "I don't like that guy. I don't like him. He's mean without reason."

Nodding with similar resentment, Everett studied D.G.'s face, but didn't say anything about the diary.

"He used to cut me down last year," D.G. said, his face red and sweaty. "I don't like kids like him. You and he really used to be best friends?"

"Sort of."

Shifting on his feet, D.G. rubbed his sneaker toe in the dirt. "Come on, let's go down by Linc and Tina's. Maybe they've moved in by now."

They walked on in silence when D.G. suddenly said, "Would you ever want to be friends with Chuck and Stuart again, if they wanted you to?"

Everett sighed. "I don't know. I'm beginning to think he's not such a good guy."

D.G. nodded and said quietly. "You're not a coward, Everett, no matter what he says."

Everett's throat suddenly felt hard and lumpy, but he forced a smile and said, "Let's go find Linc and Tina."

12
The Forest

Linc and Tina arrived late that afternoon, and the next day they were ready to go. In the early morning, the foursome stood at the big oak by Rocky Creek. D.G. had on shorts and a RUTGERS T-shirt. His blue backpack lay at the foot of the tree.

"Why don't you climb it, Everett?" D.G. said, examining the oak. "I bet you can see for miles."

Linc and Tina were also dressed in cutoff shorts as was Everett. They watched as Everett spread his hands to get a good grip on the creases in the oak bark. In a few seconds he reached the first branch and pulled himself up.

"How high do you think I can go?" he called to D.G. on the ground.

"I don't know. See how high you can get."

Winding his way up the branches, Everett didn't look down until he'd climbed for a few minutes. When he did, he almost slipped off the branch from dizziness. He had ascended a good twenty feet.

"See anything?" called D.G.

Everett turned and looked into the woods. "Too many leaves," he yelled down. "Let me go a little higher."

The branches were getting smaller and some were dead. Everett avoided them. He climbed another ten feet. The other three kids were almost hidden below him in the leaves and branches.

"Tell us!" shouted D.G. "What do you see?"

Everett smiled as his eyes swept the forest. Suddenly he felt important. It was a nice feeling. On the far edge of the trees to the south, he could see another development going up. On the western side the trees seemed to go on for miles. But he saw and heard the major highway—Route 298—farther down. He followed the brown thread of the creek as it wound around through the trees seemingly going nowhere.

"It's mostly trees," he shouted down to D.G. "You want to come up?"

D.G. didn't answer.

He searched the bottom of the tree, then spotted the three of them running up the hill to Linc and Tina's house.

After going inside, Linc came out with a rope over his shoulders.

The three raced down the hill, and D.G. called up to Everett, "Come on down to a lower branch." He pointed. It was about eight feet up, but not over the water. "You can put the rope up."

Everett began climbing down, but it was always harder going down than going up. Soon he reached the bottom branch.

"You can see everything," he said. "It's great."

"Can I come up?" asked Tina.

"Sure."

D.G. showed her how to grasp the lines in the bark. Everett watched the top of her head bob back and forth and noticed her reddish blonde hair was pulled back and tied with a bow.

He smiled as she doggedly hung on and toughed it up. A moment later, she stood with him on the branch, grinning. "See, I can do this stuff."

"Never thought you couldn't," Everett replied.

"Okay, we'll throw you the rope," D.G. said, interrupting. "Tie it on that branch hanging out over the water. You know how to make a knot, maybe a bowline or something? Don't fall in love, now."

As Tina blushed, Everett just rolled his eyes. He knew how to tie a bowline from visiting his grandfather's cabin in the Pennsylvania Poconos. They had a boat and Gramp had taught him all the sailing knots.

The branch D.G. wanted him to use was about five feet above the branch he and Tina stood on. It was thick at the base and hung out well over the water. Everett sized it up and thought it looked solid. He shouldn't have any trouble.

"Okay, throw up the rope."

Looping the rope expertly, Linc swung it in his hand and shot it up toward Everett and Tina. The rope played out and Tina grabbed an end as it soared over her head.

Everett grabbed the rope and climbed the five feet to the branch. Then he straddled it and sat down. He shimmied out on it until he sat free over the water. Swallowing, Everett calmed the shaking in his arms. Hanging out alone on it that way had an unnerving effect. He stopped and swayed to see if the branch sagged. It didn't move.

"It'll hold," said D.G. "Be tough. Think like an Israeli."

Everett murmured to himself. "Easy for you to say."

He held the rope in his right hand and pulled himself farther out on the branch. He was about six feet out now. "How far do you want me to go?"

Squinting, D.G. wrinkled his nose. "Keep going. We have to get far enough out so it can swing all the way to the other side."

As he moved farther out over the water, Everett felt sweaty and dizzy. Twice he closed his eyes and breathed slowly to quiet himself. The branch began to dip a little. He worried that if he went much farther he would slip off.

"Are you all right, Everett?" Tina called.

He shook his head. "Just a little dizzy. I'm okay."

"Just about three more feet," D.G. shouted.

Everett knew he could easily slip around the branch if he wasn't careful. He was also afraid it might crack. He listened intently for any sounds indicating it would break. But though he could bounce slightly on the branch, it seemed solid.

"I don't think I can go much farther."

D.G. and Linc stepped back and talked quietly. Finally, D.G. said, "Okay, we'll try it there. But you might have to go back up."

Everett bit his lip. There was no way he was doing that. His face felt clammy, and he was on edge. They had to get it right the first time. He said, "Maybe this isn't the right branch." He looked up briefly to see if there were any others that might work. There were none.

"No, that's the only one," D.G. answered. "See if you can make one more foot. Then tie the rope there."

The rope hung down to the ground where Linc gripped it in his hand. Linc said, "I don't think he should go any farther. Just put it there."

Everett shook his head. "No. Let's do it right. I can make another crummy foot."

He shimmied carefully along the tree branch. One inch. Two inches. Man, this was slow. The stream below him looked like a mile away.

"There," D.G. shouted. "That's far enough. I'm sure. Put it there."

Panting, Everett felt as though he was hanging by a thread over a pit. He mechanically wrapped the rope four times around the branch, then began tying a bowline. As he bent forward to tie it, he linked his feet under him. All he needed was to slip and he'd be done for.

Finally he got the bowline in place.

D.G. shook the rope slightly. "Great. Now move back."

Shimmying backward, Everett instantly knew he was in trouble. His pants were snagged on a broken branch. He lifted to pull himself off it, but as he did he began to slip.

"I'm stuck," he shouted. His heart began hammering, and he glanced at Tina, a surge of panic rising in his chest.

13
Seemed like a Mile Down

Suddenly, Tina cried out, "Be careful, Everett. Be really careful."

"See if you can lift up just a little over it," shouted D.G.

Everett pushed. The snag was tight. What on earth was it?

He pushed again, but he couldn't budge. He looked down. The ground seemed to sizzle underneath him, the way things look when you watched them behind a hot fire.

Then his sweaty hands slipped on the bark. He began to slide around. In desperation, Everett lunged and smashed his face and hands to the limb, wrapping his arms around the tree limb. His pants didn't seem to be caught anymore. But now his behind was edging down around the edge of the limb.

He knew if he didn't do something, he would go over, caught underneath the branch. He hugged the branch more tightly. But he couldn't hold it. Then he heard something rip. His shorts.

Then it happened. He slipped all the way over. Everyone was shouting somewhere underneath him and the air went out of him. He hung upside down under the branch, holding on by his arms. He felt dizzy, weary. "Just let go," something inside him whispered. But his mind shrieked to hold on. His right leg was still over the limb, holding on, but his left leg dangled uselessly. He told himself just to hold, to hold on tight, it would be all right.

Then he heard a voice. It seemed to come out of the sky. Or was it below him?

"Grab the rope, Everett. Grab the rope."

"Which way?" Everett said, his voice muffled by the closeness of the branch. He opened his eyes. He could see the sky spread out above him like a huge blanket.

"Just a foot away," said D.G, his voice still and smooth. "You can slide down. Just shimmy a foot."

Everett couldn't see anything but the sky and the underside of the branch. He swung his left leg up to hug the branch, but he couldn't get a hold. He kept his right leg hung over the branch on the other side.

Inching forward, he found a bump on the top of the

branch and clutched it with his right hand. It occurred to him to use his left hand to grab the rope. "All right," he murmured. "This is okay." Slowly, he pulled himself around with his right leg and his hand.

"Grab the rope!" shouted D.G.

"We'll all hold it!" yelled Tina, now on the ground. "You can slide down."

Everett breathed out. *I have to let go with my left hand and grab the rope*, he thought. *I can hold it with my right.*

He let go.

His body dropped.

He whipped out with his left hand. Where was the rope?

Flailing, he felt it strike the back of his hand. He grabbed it. At the same time, he swung around, pulling his leg off the branch. His body hurtled sideways. Scissoring the rope with his legs, he slid down. His hands burned. Tina and Linc pulled the rope, holding it tight.

A second later he hit the ground and fell into a heap.

He felt dizzy and nauseous, but suddenly he realized someone was close to his face. The first thing Everett was aware of was the big red blotch on D.G.'s cheek. "You okay, Everett?" the boy asked anxiously.

Everett squinted up at the three faces. They were blurry. "Let me stand up." His heart seemed to be hammering through his shirt.

Two strong hands grabbed him under his armpits and pulled him to his feet. His legs felt wobbly.

Holding him up, D.G. said, "Everybody back. Give him room to breathe."

Everett shook his head again. His mind was clearing.

"You'll be all right. Just breathe regularly," D.G. said, forcing Everett to walk.

Slowly, the blurriness went away. He didn't feel as dizzy anymore. He hobbled forward. Then another step. D.G. had his arm around his shoulders.

"I'm okay," Everett said suddenly. "I'm okay."

D.G. chuckled. "Hey, that was fantastic. From now on we call you 'Spider!' "

A grin forming on his face, Everett sighed noisily.

"You were great," Tina cried. "I was afraid you were going to fall into the creek."

"Yeah, we thought you were done for," said Linc.

"Never," said D.G. with finality. "Spider's indestructible."

They walked around in circles on the grass until Everett felt calm.

Finally, D.G. said, "Let's all sit down." Everett noticed how his legs and palms burned.

"I'll go get something for your cuts," said Tina, as she jumped up. "You're all scratched up."

Everett sat there while D.G. and Linc tried to tell jokes.

"What do you get if you cross a mosquito and a rabbit?" said D.G.

No one answered. "Bugs Bunny."

Everett couldn't help but laugh, even though it hurt.

"How do you catch a u-neek-ee bird?" asked Linc.

"You neek up on it," said Linc. They all groaned.

When Tina returned, red-faced and out of breath, everyone was still laughing.

"D.G. has the worst jokes," said Linc.

"No worse than yours," answered D.G.

Tina held out a can to begin spraying. "Quit laughing and help Everett," Tina said disapprovingly.

Everett held out his hands. The spray felt cool and refreshing. After Tina finished, he lay back on the grass and looked up at the sky. When everyone had rested, D.G. said, "If everyone's ready, we have a forest to explore." He looked at Everett. "You okay, Spider?"

Everett nodded. He was just glad to be on the ground.

D.G. and Linc stood and made a loop in the rope for their feet. "We'll have to tie it to the tree somehow so it doesn't end up always hanging over the water," said D.G. "But for now, let's see how it works. Do you want to do the honors?"

He was looking at Everett. Everett answered, "You do it. I'm wiped."

A slight wind ruffled the leaves above them. D.G. stood on the bank holding the rope. The bank rose about three or four feet above the water and ended on the other side with a similar rise. It was about ten feet across. D.G. set his foot in the loop, and with a yelp, swung across. He didn't jump off on the other side, but simply swung back.

Then Linc and Tina tried it.

After several more tries, with branches above them

groaning with the weight, D.G. put on his blue backpack and swung out over the water, then jumped off on the other side into the grass.

After Linc and Tina followed, Everett took his turn. As he swung across, everyone laughed. "What's so funny?" he cried.

Pointing to the back of his pants, Linc said, "Don't look now, but your underpants are showing a little."

"The hazards of combat," D.G. said, patting Everett on the shoulder. "But we can't let a little thing like torn shorts stop us. Come on. Let's scout this place out."

He hung the rope on a tree by the water. "We'll have to find a way of making the rope less visible. But this is okay for now."

He smiled confidently, turned, and walked jauntily into the woods.

All morning they scouted out the area just across the creek. After going back home for lunch, Everett invited them to come over and play in his basement. They built a fort out of several large boxes and even let Lance and Jillie play with them. Everett's mother met all of them for the first time. She even brought down some Kool-Aid and apple pie.

Later in the afternoon, they played football in the field behind Everett's house. Everett and Linc showed D.G. and Tina how to tackle a runner when he was coming at you and running away from you.

That night as Everett watched television, he overheard

his mother and father talking about the news—how the president was handling a crisis in the banking industry, the turmoil in Russia, and more about the local electronics thieves the police were looking for.

Everett wondered why parents were so interested in news all the time. "I guess I'll be like that when I grow up," he said with a sigh and turned back to the TV, not really interested. "Indiana Jones" was much more captivating.

At bedtime, Everett complained that his rope burns hurt, and his mother made him take a long bath. When he was done, his father came in to say good-night. Everett told him how he and his new friends planned to explore the woods.

His dad looked at Everett seriously and said, "Ev, are things really going okay?"

"They're all right."

"Good. Anything change with Chuck and Stuart?"

"Not really." Everett sensed his dad's concern, but somehow he wasn't sure how much Chuck and Stewart mattered anymore.

When his father went out, Everett put his hands behind his head and watched the lights from passing cars slash along the ceiling. He wondered if there was any way he and Chuck would ever be friends again. And if they were, would D.G. be included? And Linc and Tina?

He chewed his lip and listened to Lance's breathing in the bed next to him. He knew now that he would never desert D.G., or even Linc or Tina. They were friends now—

for good. No matter what Chuck said. Still, he wished somehow he could bring them all together.

Finally, he rolled over and murmured, "Why do things have to be so complicated?"

For a long time, he couldn't sleep, but suddenly it was morning and his mother was standing over him.

"Wake up, Evvie. It's time to get going."

14
Butterscotch Cupcakes

D.G. was already swinging on the rope when Everett arrived at the creek the next day. He wore his blue back-pack again. Everett had begun wearing a backpack too, to put things in, like a Scout knife, some potato chips, and a joke book.

Moments later, Tina and Linc arrived and were ready to go.

There weren't any visible trails in among the trees, so D.G. had to forge his own way forward. He pushed brush and brambles out of the way as they made their path. It was cool that morning, quiet, no insects buzzing around. Birds chirped around them and an occasional squirrel scrabbled up a tree.

They followed Rocky Creek downstream. But there were too many brambles. As they walked farther into the woods, they found the forest floor was fairly clear of bushes. Here lots of trees grew tall, with a thick bed of dead leaves around the trunks.

Deeper in the woods, D.G. suddenly stopped everyone to listen. "Maybe we'll hear something important," he said. Everett knew there was a deserted house farther up along a back road that he and Chuck had seen over a year ago. They hadn't gone in, but he wondered if it was still there.

The four of them stood there breathing as quietly as they could. In the distance, they heard the high-pitched whir of a chain saw. But there were no other sounds, except birds and the wind through the leaves.

"Come on," said D.G. "Maybe we can find some interesting stuff back here. Maybe there'll be some haunted houses, or an old dam, or a harem of giants, or something."

Harem, Everett thought. *A harem of giants?* He laughed as he followed D.G. and Tina.

They wandered along through the woods until they found a trail leading away from the creek.

"Let's follow this," D.G. suggested. "It's got to go somewhere. Maybe to the Gobi Desert or someplace." He turned and hoisted his backpack a little, crinkled his smile, then trudged forward.

"What've you got in your backpack?" asked Everett.

"Stuff," said D.G. as he turned to head up the trail.

"What kind of stuff?"

"Good stuff," said D.G. He turned and smiled slyly at everyone. "Stuff that will quiver your liver. Now let's get going."

Everett wondered why D.G. had to be so secretive sometimes. Usually he liked it, but right now he wanted to know what was in the pack.

Tina said, "Do you think we should get so far from the creek?"

"We won't get lost," Everett answered. "Just follow the sun. I've been back here before, anyway."

She squinted up at the tops of the trees, where streams of sunlight filtered through, and shrugged. Linc followed, murmuring, "Just don't get into any poison ivy." They wound through the woods. Skunk cabbage grew everywhere. A squishy sound came with each step. It was darker. The cool air refreshed their faces, and the swampy smell of the woods right near the creek disappeared.

Soon they reached higher ground. Sunlight broke through the trees above them in places, and Everett arched his back into the warmth.

D.G. led. Then Everett, Tina, and Linc. Everett fingered his slingshot and checked his pocket. He had put four stones in there earlier. Just in case, he told himself. The trail steepened and a clearing appeared ahead. Then they reached the edge of the woods and found a dirt road, overgrown with weeds. Fresh tire tracks were printed neatly on it. Some car or truck left the weeds bent in two parallel lines.

Panting, they all stopped and looked back and forth. The road disappeared in each direction into the trees, with no landmarks visible. D.G. knelt and yanked up a yellow flower. "Buttercups," he said. "Let's see who likes butter."

He held the buttercup underneath Tina's chin. Everett saw a shiny patch of light beam onto her chin. "Tina does!"

Moving from one to the other, D.G. exclaimed, "Everyone likes butter!"

"What about you?" Everett said playfully.

"Definitely," said D.G. "In fact . . . " He hefted the backpack off his back. "Just to prove it, I have something with a little butter in it."

A moment later, D.G. produced four packs of butterscotch cupcakes.

"Fantastic!" Linc declared.

They all crowded around. "Where did you get them?" asked Tina.

"My mom. She has millions of them. We keep a big stock. My dad works for a big bakery company in Phillie."

Everett remembered how Mrs. Frankl offered him some at D.G.'s house the time he was there. "Do you get them for free?" he asked, his eyes wide. Now why didn't his father have a job like that?

"As many as we want," said D.G. "There's more where these came from." He handed a pack to each of them. "But we only get one pack each for now. Sometimes my mom is sort of a cupcake miser." He chuckled, unwrapped the paper, and bit into one.

Everett did the same and chomped off a hunk.

"Wait!" said D.G., as he glanced around at them. "You're not eating it right."

They all stopped and stared at him. How could you not eat a butterscotch cupcake right?

"You eat it upside down," said D.G. "That way the icing touches your tongue first. The flavor really zooms in that way. Try it."

Looking at each other, they all cautiously turned over their cupcakes and bit in. The moment the creamy, butterscotch frosting touched Everett's tongue, little jolts of pleasure shot through his mouth. "It's great!" he exclaimed.

"Definitely," said D.G. with a lopsided grin.

They sat down and devoured the cupcakes. D.G put the wrappers back into his knapsack. "Shouldn't litter," he explained.

Finishing, D.G. pulled on the pack. "Okay, which way?" he said looking at the road and then the other three.

Everett had been as far as the house before, but he didn't know what was beyond it. "There's a deserted house down that way," he said, pointing to the arm of the road that went to the right.

"Let's do it," said D.G. He stepped off briskly and everyone followed. The sunlight beat down on their heads, and Everett felt happy. Quietly he hummed a tune he remembered from Scouts: "The ants went marching one by one, hurrah, hurrah . . ." Soon he was singing out loud and everyone joined him till the woods seemed to resound with their voices.

15
The Run-down House

They marched up the road to the house. Everett had never been inside. It was scary looking, run down, and looking at it always made him shiver inside.

As they trekked along, the singing died and suddenly, Tina tapped Everett's arm. "He's not going to do something bad, is he?"

Everett shook his head. "No, it's just an old house. Don't worry."

She wrinkled her brow with concern, though, as D.G. continued down the little road without speaking. Everyone was quiet. You could almost hear the air vibrate it was so still. It felt hot and sticky. Everett suddenly wished they could just go back and forget the whole thing.

But D.G. was obviously interested. And when that happened, there was no turning back. The smaller road to the house was overgrown, cutting through the trees in a winding path.

"This is giving me the creeps," said Tina.

D.G. turned and grinned mischievously. "It's supposed to. Guess we'll just have to find out what's at the end of the road."

There were fresh tire tracks on the dirt surface. The sky was clouding over now, and the woods began to darken. D.G. took the first step onto the grassy hump in the middle of the road.

Everett looked at Tina and Linc. "What should we do?"

Linc shook his head. "Let's go on. It can't hurt anything."

Glancing nervously at Tina, Everett told himself to be cool. But Tina chewed her lip anxiously. After another look around, they all began following Linc and D.G. up the pathway.

Five minutes later they reached a clearing. D.G. motioned everyone to get down. Ahead of them stood the gray, wind-worn house. There was a shack out back that looked like a garage. No car was visible. No person appeared at a window or in the yard. D.G. said, "I don't know whether anyone lives here, but I think we should find out."

Everett scrutinized the house. Did they have to go right up to it? He listened intently for any sound.

"This is our plan," said D.G. "We sneak up and get around the building. Once we've cleared it for human presence, we try to get inside."

"But what if someone lives there?" said Tina. "We could get into a lot of trouble." She looked at Everett and Linc for support.

"That's what we have to find out," said D.G., his eyes squinty and hard, but glittering with pleasure. "Who knows? Maybe some monster lives in there. Or some man with a hump. Or a vampire. Or a . . . " D.G. made a face like a vampire.

"D.G., you're scaring me," said Tina through clenched teeth.

"Oh, relax," D.G. chided. "It's probably deserted."

Tina folded her arms. "All right. Let's get this over with."

Everett wished someone would just appear. The silence drove him crazy. He noticed two metal posts on the edge of the wood across the driveway. A broken chain lay in the dirt between the posts. Whoever owned it didn't keep the chain up.

D.G. said, "Okay, keep low. Let's go for that far edge. Be as silent as you can. No talking till we're at the house and have listened to see if anyone's there."

As Everett waited, Tina tugged on his sleeve restlessly. But he just glanced at her and put his finger to his lips. D.G. shot out ahead of them and was halfway across the clearing before anyone else moved. Then Everett ran bent down, trying to pretend he was invisible.

In a minute, all four of them stood at the house. Cracked and peeling paint tore off at a touch. There was one large window on the second floor, close to the front of the house. The panes were broken out. Then high up at the point where the two sides of the roof came together, there stood another smaller square window, open. It had no glass or screen.

It didn't really look like a window to Everett. There was a pipe up the side of the house all the way to it. He thought it might be at the end of the attic. He might even be able to climb it, if necessary. But he didn't want to do that. He wanted to leave.

D.G. stared up at the two windows on either side of the door with his hands on his hips. Everett suspected he would have to stand on someone's shoulders to look in.

Putting his finger to his lips, D.G. pointed to Everett. He mouthed the words, "You follow me," then told Linc and Tina to stay and guard the side. He crept around the house, keeping down under the window. Stooping under it, D.G. motioned that he'd need a boost to look in. Everett clasped his hands together and made a step. D.G. hopped up for a quick look.

He was only up for a moment, then jumped back down to the ground. "Looks deserted. Some crud on the floor, though. Ripped up boxes or something. We'd better check it out."

Check it out? Was he crazy?

D.G. signaled to Linc and Tina and whispered, "Come on around. It's empty."

How did he know that? Everett sighed nervously. *How far were they going to go?*

Linc and Tina joined them under the window, looking around with wide, frightened eyes. "What now?" said Tina, shivering and looking back toward the driveway in the woods. "Shouldn't we go?"

D.G. shook his head. "Yes. Go in, that is. We have to know if anyone's here." He slunk over to the door and motioned to everyone to stand up against the house and be quiet. Then he tried the door handle. It turned with a rusty rasp. D.G. glanced at the three others, took a breath, and pulled the door open. It creaked so loudly that D.G. jumped down and lay back dramatically against the front of the house.

That was enough for the others. First Tina, then Linc, and finally Everett took off for the road. But when they got to the two metal posts, they turned around and saw D.G. standing in front of the door with his hands on his hips, shaking his head with disgust. He waved to them to come back. Everett looked at Linc and Tina and they both rolled their eyes.

"This is a real horror show," said Tina.

"I know," said Everett. "But we shouldn't leave D.G. there all alone."

They all hurried back to where D.G. was. He whispered, "What's the matter?"

Everett gave him a fierce look. "What do you think's the matter?"

"There's nothing to worry about," D.G. said. "Now stand on either side of the door in case something comes out."

"In case something comes out!" Tina almost shouted. "Like what?"

Grimacing and putting his finger to his lips, D.G. said, "A werewolf maybe. I don't know. We have to stare the monster in the face and spit in his eye. That's the only way to overcome fear." This time when he twisted the door handle, no one ran. But Everett's heart was pounding.

With an expressive grin, D.G. threw the door open, then jumped to the side. He lay up against the side of the house as the door swung all the way around, squeaking like a burned rat. It knocked into the front wall.

Nothing else happened. Everett wondered if D.G. was scared or just pretending. He had to be one of the best pretenders Everett had ever met. D.G. poked his head around the door jamb and looked in. After twisting and checking and whistling twice, D.G. said, "Come on. It's empty. We'll have to scope out the whole building."

Everyone stared at him, astonished. "You mean we have to go in?" Everett croaked.

D.G. gave him a look like he was the crazy one. "Definitely," he said. "That's what we're all here for."

Chewing his lip nervously, and not knowing whether to run, scream, or crumple to the ground, Everett looked at Linc again. Linc's face was white. Tina's arms were all goose flesh and she kept looking off toward the road. But D.G. jumped up and stood in the doorway. "Let's go men . . . and women," he boomed. "This is what separates the commandos from the chicken hearts."

He disappeared inside. Everett knew he wasn't staying outside without D.G. so he jumped up on the stoop and followed. Tina and Linc were right behind him, all of them pressed together and bumping into each other.

The house was cooler inside and had a musty, damp smell. In the room to the right a few ripped-open boxes lay, torn up and stained. Cigarette butts dotted the floor, crumpled up or stubbed out. They didn't look old. Some of the floorboards were ripped out, and the flooring appeared rotten. D.G. knelt down and picked up a butt. There were several red and white smashed up packets on the floor, too. "Marlboros," said D.G. "Whatever lives here smokes Marlboros."

Tina suddenly seethed, "We don't know that anyone lives here, D.G. Will you quit saying that!"

Sighing, D.G. said, "Anyway, this room's clean. No werewolves here." He bent down to the floorboards. But it was too dark to see into the black regions below.

He looked up at Everett. "Do you want to split up, or should we all go together?"

Everett couldn't believe he could ask such a question.

As he started to answer, there was a loud creak. The whole house shook. Tina and Linc turned and backed up toward the door, as though to run, but they didn't.

But after a moment of listening, D.G. said, "It's just the wind. Don't worry. It's all right. But I think we should all stick together and not split up. Okay?"

No one answered until Tina gave D.G. a terrified look. "We're all staying together," she said, her voice shaking. "I'm not going anywhere in here alone."

Everett detected a hint of a smile on D.G.'s lips, but it quickly passed and D.G. turned toward the next doorway. That room was mostly vacant except for cigarette butts and more crumpled packets. Some newspapers lay around too, and D.G. picked up one to look at the date. "Over six weeks old," he said and handed it to Everett. "Someone was here at least six weeks ago. Or maybe less." He winked at Tina. She looked away and hissed with exasperation.

The stairs stood straight ahead. Next was a hallway. The wallpaper hung on the walls, some peeled off and curled in strips. Brown splotches stained it, as if someone had been chewing tobacco and spitting it onto the walls.

"Linc, you guard the stairs," D.G. said, "in case something comes down. Everett, Tina, and I will see what's in back."

Linc grabbed D.G.'s arm. "I'm not staying here. What might come down?"

Poking him in the back, Everett said, "Just come on. Don't listen to him. We're all staying together."

Creeping down the passageway, the three of them followed D.G. into the back. It was an ancient kitchen. An old copper sink lay there bent and beat up next to an antique-looking refrigerator. The windows above it were broken. D.G. ran his hand along the tabletop, with knife-cut initials all over it. Cigarette butts cluttered the floor amid some dried mud shoe tracks on the floor.

"It wears hiking boots," said D.G. with an amazed expression. "See."

He bent down and pointed to a track on the floor. "Maybe it's a Boy Scout," he said. But no one laughed. Tina crossed her arms and looked as though she was going to either cry or scream.

To the right of the kitchen hung a door with a rusted combination lock on it. Clearly, someone *had* been using the house. Everett vaguely thought of the thieves his father had spoken about, but that seemed impossible. Why would they come out here? Still, those were empty tape deck and stereo boxes in the front room.

"Probably a cellar," said D.G. He gazed at the other three. "We should probably find out what's in it. What do you think?"

Tina's eyes popped. "No way we're going down there."

Giving her his amazed, "What—don't-you-trust-me?" look, D.G. said, "I don't know. We should probably check it out. There might even be dead bodies in it."

Tina sucked in her breath noisily and glared at D.G., then shook her head.

"Next time we come," D.G. said, "we'll bring a crowbar so we can get into the cellar. But what's over here?"

There was a door to the right and a little porch. Two broken chairs lay in a pile on the floor. On top of a table sat a balled-up plastic bag with what looked like seasoning in it. D.G. picked it up. He breathed out loudly. "Look at this. Could it be drugs or something?"

He handed the bag to Everett. He didn't know. He'd never seen anything like it, and he wasn't going to smell it.

"Any of you ever seen drugs?" said D.G.

Everyone shook their heads.

"Neither have I. Maybe we ought to take it as evidence."

With a frown, Everett took it out of D.G.'s hand and placed the bag back on the table. "We're leaving everything like we found it. There've been people here. Who knows what they're doing here?"

D.G. nodded. "Yeah, I agree. We don't want them to know we've been here."

"Who's them?" Tina said again.

"The werewolves," D.G. said matter-of-factly.

"I hate this, D.G.," Tina said. "I really hate it. I think we should go." She looked at Everett and Linc.

Linc just shrugged. "I'm getting used to it now."

Meanwhile D.G. looked around at everyone. "Don't you see? This is a test of courage. If we can't get through this, we can't get through anything. So let's just do it. Then we'll all know."

"Know what?" Tina seethed.

"That none of us wets his pants when things get tough," D.G. said, his eyes wide and confident.

Everett sighed and noticed Tina and Linc looking at D.G. with wonder and worry, but they continued walking through the house.

There was nothing else in the back. The porch was enclosed, but someone had torn out the screens. The door was off its hinge and skewed against the wall.

"Okay, this is all clean. Let's go upstairs," said D.G.

This time Everett protested loudly. "No way, no way, no way! We're leaving." That was where the creak had come from. He remembered an old movie that had a scene where this ancient, crazy person sat upstairs in a rocking chair. And the person was just bones—dead! That was enough for him. What if there was something like that here? What if the person who smoked the cigarettes sat up there— waiting? With a knife or a huge dog or something?

Walking around them, D.G. rolled his eyes, and went to the base of the stairs. "Don't be such mambies," he said with mock disgust. "What are you—men or bunny rabbits?"

Sighing, Everett and the others followed mechanically. He told himself just to go along, it was all right, there was nothing to be scared of. But deep down he didn't believe a word of it. All houses had something. And you never knew about it until it bit into you.

They stood at the base of the stairs. Everett felt Tina's breath on his neck. She grabbed onto his belt.

D.G. said, "Watch out for rotten stairs when we go up. Be real careful." Everett decided not even to protest. If D.G. had ice in his blood, so did he.

D.G. tested the first stair. It was sturdy. He took it one stair at a time, testing each one. Everett kept his ears pricked for the slightest noise. But D.G. kept going up. As he stepped on each stair it squeaked noisily.

When they were halfway up, the whole house shifted and creaked again in the wind. D.G. stayed cool as an ice pack. As they reached the top, Everett noticed something on the floor. D.G. picked it up.

"Hey, it's an old-time picture."

It was a snapshot of a family. It looked like a Civil War-type photo Everett remembered from some of his father's history books. The picture was torn on the edge, and the glass covering had shattered. A picture of a harsh looking family stared out at them.

"They all must have had bad hemorrhoids," D.G. said.

Everyone chuckled nervously. D.G. went on, "Maybe they're the people who lived here before . . ."

Not completing the sentence, D.G. stared into each face.

"Before?" Tina said uneasily.

"Before the things got them that came up out of the basement," he said with a raise of his eyebrows. Everett could see now how much D.G. was enjoying this. How could he be so cool? Everett wondered.

D.G. walked over to the first room and peered in. Everett stood in the doorway, ready to bolt if necessary. Tina and Linc hung behind him. Everett saw more newspaper clippings lying around, one about the president, another about war in Iraq, and several other headlines about local crime.

"Come on in," said D.G., surveying the walls. "It's okay. There's nothing here."

Everett finally pushed himself past the doorway and looked into the rooms on the top floor. There was a small washroom in the middle. But no tub or toilet.

A larger bedroom stood on the right side over the porch, with two smaller bedrooms on the left side. D.G. picked up another newspaper lying on the floor of the room on the right side.

"Look at this," he whispered. "It's the employment section. Werewolves looking for employment? That's amazing."

Everett wished he could laugh, but his stomach was too tight. "Who cares?" he said. "Let's just get out of here." He kept listening for any noises.

D.G. sighed. "Okay, this place is clean. Let's go." He looked up at a ceiling hatch which was open. "Should we go up into the attic?"

Everett shook his head. "I think we should just go."

"Yeah," said D.G. "Probably nothing up there but all the bodies."

Tina rolled her eyes, but everyone breathed a sigh of relief. At least he wasn't going to make them do that, Everett thought.

They headed down the stairs. Suddenly, a strange, violent rattle shook through the house from the breeze. All four of them leaped to the bottom of the stairs in a jumble and sprinted out the front door. They didn't stop till they were out at the main road.

A moment later, they were all laughing. "Man, did you scare me, D.G.!" Linc said.

Tina was shaking her head and laughing, "I never want to do that again, but it was fun."

Everett noticed how cool D.G. remained. How could he be like that? But deep down inside he admired him. He wondered what D.G. would write in his diary about it.

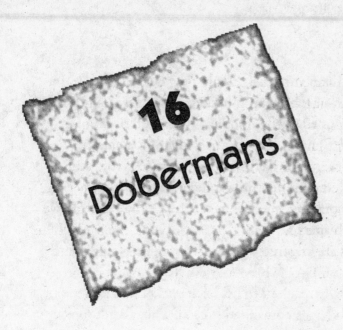

16
Dobermans

They ambled on down the road, talking fast with relief and release. Linc suggested they go home, but D.G. wanted to see what was around the bend, about two hundred feet ahead.

The sun burned on their foreheads. Everyone was hot and sticky. Everett's legs itched from brushing against all the weeds. There were flecks of seeds and white dandelion fluff all over him. The smell of the clay road and the undergrowth hinted goldenrod and new-mown hay.

As D.G. led, Everett stretched and the farther they got from the driveway to the house, the better he felt. But as he relaxed, D.G.'s voice suddenly rang out. "Freeze!"

Two dogs—Doberman pinschers—trotted around the bend and stopped in the middle of the road, staring at them. Everett's heart leapt and he caught his breath. Dobermans were the worst. Everyone stood statue still.

Tina edged over next to Everett. Out of the corner of his eye, he could see she was as terrified as he. "Should we run?" she whispered.

"Stand still," Everett said. "If we run, they may come after us."

D.G. slowly reached to his back pocket and pulled out his sling. The dogs continued staring. They didn't look especially mean. But no one else moved.

D.G. whispered out of the side of his mouth. "Get a stone ready, everyone."

Holding his breath, Everett inched his hand up to his pocket and drew out the slingshot as furtively as he could. Then he grabbed a stone.

The dogs still stared, panting and looking about peaceably. One sat back on his haunches and scratched his belly with a rear paw. D.G. backed up, moving his feet as slowly as possible. "Walk evenly," he said quietly.

Suddenly, the dogs were up and barking, still hesitating about what to do. Tina turned to run. Linc followed. Everett wanted to run, but he knew he couldn't desert D.G. Then with a loud double bark, the dogs leapt forward. They galloped toward the foursome.

D.G. stopped and whirled his sling, standing his ground.

The dogs were less than a hundred feet away now. Everett twisted in position as Tina shouted, "Run!"

He knew the sling wouldn't do any good. But he couldn't just leave D.G. there in the road. He jammed the stone in the pouch and circled it over his head.

Then a deep-throated voice bellowed, "Whip! Bump! Stop!"

The two dogs nearly fell over one another. They turned abruptly and galloped back to a big, barrel-chested man in the middle of the road. He wore a gray hunter's cap, long blue jean farmer's pants, and a short-sleeved green T-shirt. It was The Jackal!

The dogs jumped around at his feet, then turned and faced the four kids, as though to say, "Look what we found."

The Jackal called out to them, "It's all right, boys and girls. Whip and Bump won't do anything. They're just playin'."

D.G. stuffed his sling back in his pocket. "Come on. It's The Jackal. Let's meet him again."

Tina and Linc stopped and ran back up behind Everett. Tina's face glistened with sweat. "You know him?"

"Sort of," said Everett with a sigh of relief. He folded the sling and put it back into his side pocket.

The Jackal grinned at D.G. as he walked up. "Well, if it isn't David the shepherd, about to use his sling on one of my children. At least it's not a bulldozer!" He grinned broadly.

"We didn't know you lived back here," D.G. said.

"Well, I wasn't about to tell you all, seein' you probably would want to get in my truck and drive it."

As they ran up to D.G. and the man, Everett told Linc and Tina about how they'd met him at the school. The two dogs jostled in among the four and gave each a sniff. Everett held up his hands, but when Tina petted one, he put them down and touched the bigger dog. Soon, they'd given everyone a lick. D.G. introduced the others.

"What's your real name?" D.G. said.

"What did you call me that day?"

D.G. grinned sheepishly, then hung his head a little. "The Jackal."

The big man laughed heartily. He seemed a lot different from their first encounter. "Well, my real name's Seth Williamson. You can call me Seth." He held out his hand. "It's nice to meet you when you're not getting into trouble. Or are you?" He eyed them skeptically, then clapped D.G. on the back, "You all look kinda hot. Would you like some of my homemade iced tea? I bet you're all drier then a painted broomstick in a box factory."

Everett smiled, remembering how Seth used strange expressions when he talked. He thought some iced tea would be fine. Real fine.

17
Seth's Place

They walked on for another hundred yards and came to a little cut in the trees. There, back from the dirt road, stood a little cabin. It was a tidy little place, with a large woodpile, a battered truck in the front that Everett now remembered seeing at the school, and a small, newly planted garden. The woodsy area looked clean and well kept. The front of the house had a porch with two huge rosebushes on either side of the stoop. White and yellow blossoms burst from the greenery. There were several spools of green wire lying on the ground, and some chalk and pinking shears.

"This is it," said Seth, smiling. "Home sweet home."

He told Bump to go around back and get "the stick." Bump ran off behind the shack. In a moment he trotted back with a thick stick in his mouth.

"You kids can get used to these two whippersnappers with some stick throwing. It's a lot better than firing a stone between their eyes."

He gazed at them with dark brown, twinkly eyes and laughed. "Whip and Bump are good protection, too. But if they know I'm all right with you, then you're all right with them. Get my meanin'?"

Everyone nodded.

Then Seth said to the dogs, "You sit now, young fellas. Be as still as chipmunks on the edge of a cracker barrel." The two dogs sat back and waited. Seth side-armed the stick out into the road.

The two dogs glanced at it, then gazed at Seth, waiting for the command. Then, Seth bellowed, "Bump!" The Doberman leaped forward, barking and yowling. He raced to the woods, jerked up the stick in his teeth, and pranced back, dropping it at Seth's feet.

"Whip!" Seth shouted again.

Whip picked up the dropped stick, and ran it back out into the middle of the road. He stood there, panting and waiting for the next command.

"Let 'er rip!" boomed Seth.

Instantly, Whip leaped in an angle backwards, flinging the stick over his head. It sailed into the woods on the far side of the road. Then Seth said quietly, "Bump."

This time Bump darted out and grabbed up the stick with a snarl. Bringing it back to Seth, the dog shook it in his mouth and then dropped it at Seth's feet. After giving Bump a pat on the head, he said, "Ball."

Again Bump jumped up, skittered around the edge of the house, and picked up a green tennis ball lying in the dirt. He brought it back and laid it at Seth's feet.

It was a regular circus. Everett watched in amazement. The dogs seemed to know every trick imaginable. But after a few minutes, Seth said, "Okay, boys, play now. I'm hotter than a gnat under an empty pickle jar in the Sahara at twelve o' one in the middle of a summer still storm."

Everyone laughed. D.G. said, "Now that's hot."

Seth smiled. "Oh, you'll get used to my expressions. I have lots of them."

The two dogs nosed the ball back and forth, then stood there panting and watching everyone.

"You got to teach dogs to have fun with themselves. Otherwise, they're trailing you right into the outhouse. Can't sit on the can without four eyes staring up into your belly button." Everyone laughed again and Seth smiled affectionately on the two dogs as they waited out in the road. Seth let them all play with the dogs for a few more minutes, then D.G. said, "How long have you lived here, Seth?"

"Almost since Noah's flood," said Seth, rolling his eyes with a merry twinkle. He turned to go into the cabin. As

Everett looked at it again, it didn't look as much like a cabin anymore as a comfortable little house. It had brown shutters on the sides, a green, shingled roof, windows on either side of the door, and a rocking chair on the porch.

When no one moved, Seth turned and said, "Well, you comin' in or are you goin' to stand there like the last four leaves of a maple tree this side 'a winter?"

D.G. glanced around, then raised his eyebrows and shrugged. Everyone followed him into the house. Everett hoped Seth wasn't some kind of weirdo or anything and they'd end up cooking in a big pot in the middle of the fireplace.

The house had a rustic air, one room with a table and chairs, a fireplace and kitchen, some pictures on the walls, green curtains over the windows, a large bed to the left with a quilt, and drying clothing that hung on hangers along a wall. Two big deer heads stared blankly out at them over the fireplace. Everett leaned back to look up at them.

"Shot 'em both two winters apart," said Seth. "In my shootin' days, that is. Don't do much anymore. My joints are like rusty hinges on a sunken ship."

Motioning to them to grab seats, Seth gave them glasses and set out the iced tea. Then he pulled out the chair at the head of the table and sank down into it. It was an armchair with deer's hooves as the arms. He rubbed his hand on the right hoof, then picked up his glass. "Guess we ought to clink, seein' this is the first time you have come to my abode."

The four picked up the glasses and everyone knocked them together in the middle of the table. Seth raised his glass and closed his eyes. "God of heaven, give these young kids long lives, joyful days, and a friend for every season. Amen."

Everyone was staring at him, but when he opened his eyes, he just smiled and said, "Drink up. You won't get any of this elsewhere."

The iced tea was fantastic. The sweet taste tingled and a hint of mint made Everett's mouth prickle. Seth also opened a bag of pretzels and dumped them into a bowl.

He began asking questions about where they lived and what they were doing in the woods. D.G. did most of the talking, though Seth had a way of including everyone in the conversation. Everett wondered what religion Seth was, if he went to church. He noticed some pictures of children on top of the dresser and figured they were his grandchildren.

The two dogs lay with crossed legs on the doorsill, watching the group talk. Everett felt comfortable in the cool air of the cabin and leaned back to listen.

"Good thing you didn't sling your stone into my children's teeth," said Seth. "They're taught to attack intruders. And I'm afraid they might have torn you to pieces." Seth had a deep, friendly voice that reminded Everett of his grandfather.

"We didn't know what to do," D.G. said. His voice had an awed tone Everett had never heard before. "If you hadn't come along, we'd've been cooked."

"Oh, they'd never attack unless I or someone they trust tell them to. But if you attack them, anything goes."

As they drank the iced tea and crunched pretzels, D.G. told Seth about how they had been exploring the woods like the Israelites did the land of milk and honey. Seth said, "Just don't go marchin' around my little abode here and make it fall down like old Joshua did at Jericho."

D.G.'s eyes lit up. "You know about Joshua?"

"It's in the Book, isn't it?" Seth said, smacking his lips with pleasure. "I know about most everything in the Book. My main reading every night."

There was a pause, then D.G.asked, "Do you ever tell stories from the Bible?"

Rubbing his knuckles proudly on his chest, Seth said, "My main hobby—telling stories from the Book. You want one?"

18
Seth's Story

Seth looked at Everett and then at the others as though he'd just caught a bear and was asking the bear whether it wanted to be set free or get eaten. "What story do you want?"

As Everett leaned forward, his heart bumped in his chest and he glanced at Tina and Linc. The way Seth talked and looked, Everett knew it was bound to be good. He searched his mind to think of the story he wanted to hear. But D.G. beat him to it. "How about David and Goliath?"

"Oh, that's a great one," Seth answered with a firm

nod. "The best." He leaned back in his chair. Then suddenly Seth was up on his feet, his eyes on fire.

"That giant stood there, his sword in his hand. He was the biggest, baddest giant anyone had ever seen. He was known to kill off a hundred in one fight. The champion, they called him. The Philistine Guillotine!"

Everyone laughed. It was already good.

"That was because he cut off so many heads, no one could even tell. That sword could clunk four heads off at once!"

Seth brought his arm around in a big sweep. He pretended to strike four heads, then watched them roll off to his right.

"He was dressed up in this thick, shiny armor and had a big helmet with a red tassel stringing from it. It was a long tassel made of human hair. One strand for every victim."

Turning majestically, Seth gave them a serious, far off, hard look. "He stood there, that huge sword in his right hand, and then he flicked it up whipping that metal through the air. You could almost hear it whistle. 'Come on,' he shouted—'Come on down, sons of God. I challenge you to fight. One on one. A duel. Just you and me.' "

Seth's eyes narrowed and his voice was just above a whisper. "They were all afraid. They were shakin' in their sandals. But then along comes little David. And when David hears it, he rears back. 'You goin' take that line off of that stinkin' old Philistine?' He says, 'I can take that big oaf. The bigger they stand, the harder they fall. That's what I say.'

"Well, everyone thinks to himself, 'This is just some loudmouthed kid.' But they didn't know God was on his side.

"After trying on King Saul's armor, David decided to use his slingshot. Just like that one D.G. has got. Hold it up, D.G."

His mouth agape, D.G. reached in his pocket and held it up.

"Yeah, just like that. A little slingshot."

Seth paused and caught his breath. Everett watched Seth's dark blue eyes. He leaned forward with anticipation. Seth knew his stuff!

"So David went down by the little stream and picked out five round stones. Just like miniballs in a musket they were. Then he ran out onto the field where that old Goliath was standing, yelling away.

"Now Goliath, he sees David trunch out onto the field and he's mad. He can't stand it. Children! They're sendin' him children. Is that all they think he is?"

Seth acted like Goliath, roaring in place like some kind of proud captain on the deck of a battleship. Everett swallowed, his eyes fixed on Seth's face.

"So he thinks, I don't need this old helmet" Seth whispered. "I'll get rid of this David right quick. So he threw it off and picked up his spear. He figured he'd put one right through David's heart!

"That old Goliath hurled that spear through the air. It was like one of those nuclear-warheaded guided missiles. It's goin' about a hundred miles an hour and headed straight for David's heart. Everyone is wonderin' if David can get out of the way.

"But, pooh, that was nothin.' David just moves one foot to the right . . . "

Seth shuffled to the right and everyone giggled. "And that spear goes sailin' by and plunks into the dirt, useless."

With a deft sweep to the right, Seth faked spitting on the spear.

"Well, that just gets Goliath madder. And he starts whippin' that sword and cussin' his head off. He says he's gonna cut up David and feed him to the birds. He's gonna roast him over a spit. He's gonna . . .

"And David's just standing there watchin'. Then he starts awhirlin' that sling.

"And it's then that Goliath realizes he doesn't have his helmet. So he just starts runnin' toward David, just like a freight train comin' down on the tied-up damsel in distress. He's gonna run David over.

"But you know what that David did?"

Seth gazed at Everett. He felt his heart jump.

"That David just ran forward, whippin' his sling, and that Goliath's roarin' down on him—and David's awhippin' and awhippin', and he says to himself, 'Don't fire till you see the whites of his eyes.' You can hear his footsteps rumblin' now, hear him wheezin' and breathin', and now he's only fifteen feet away. Rumblin' and roarin'.

"And then David shoots!"

Seth paused suddenly. Then: "WHACKO! Right between the eyes."

Seth stood there like Goliath, stock still, his eyeballs focused on the tip of his nose.

"And Goliath stops. His sword hand clunks down. He reaches up to touch his face. The whole two armies were silent as winter. And that old Goliath is standin' there, and standin' and then David just breathes out—Poooo!"

With a noisy wheeze, Seth "poooo-ed" into the air. The cabin was dead quiet as Seth showed the giant falling just by the motion of his eyes.

"So Goliath just fell over. Like a giant sequoia tree comin' down into the dirt on a Sunday afternoon. CLUNK!"

Suddenly Seth jumped as if the whole ground had shaken. Everyone jumped with him!

"Then David grabs up his sword and cuts off Goliath's head. He holds it up for all to see. By that black curly hair. Blood all drippin' down."

Seth stopped, looked around at the foursome. Everett barely dared to breathe.

Then Seth nodded and looked afar off. "And then that whole army comes runnin' down around David and they slammed off after the rest of the Philistines. They took care of them, real quick. Not a Philistine left with his choppers clickin' together."

Seth gave everyone a long stare, then breathed out, sat down, and folded his arms. "And that's the story of David and Goliath. That was when David and Jonathan became the best friends of the Bible."

D.G. jumped up with a cheer. "David and Jonathan are my favorite people in the whole Bible!"

Seth nodded. "They were good friends. Loyal. They stuck by one another. You won't find any better."

The moment Seth said it, Everett remembered how Seth had said that when he and D.G. were caught on the bulldozer.

"That's us," D.G. cried with excitement. "Me and Everett and Linc and Tina. We're like them!"

Seth smiled.

Suddenly D.G. said, "Tell us another one. About Joshua and Jericho."

Sighing, Seth shook his head. "Only one per afternoon. It plumb whickers me out. Now you all better scoot or your moms are gonna cut off your heads too."

D.G. glanced at his watch. "Ai-yi-yi! Three o'clock. My mom'll have a bird."

Everyone shuffled out, thanking Seth. He patted them all on the back and led them out. "We'll escort you to where you came out of the woods."

"Can we come again tomorrow?" asked Tina.

Seth nodded. "It's all right by me. But I do work most of the time. I just didn't work today because they had to do some special things at the school. But you better check it out with your folks first. Anyway, I usually get home about 3:30 or so."

They walked out to the spot where they'd come onto the road. Seth watched them and waved as they wound their way back into the woods.

Walking home through the woods, Linc, Tina, and D.G. chattered about the house and Seth and Seth's story. They were excited and happy. Everett trailed behind them all, thinking how good he felt. That was it. He was happy. Maybe Chuck and Stuart didn't really matter that much anymore. He had new friends, and even if he wasn't at the pool, maybe this was better.

The moment it occurred to him, he knew it was the truth.

The foursome spent several days visiting Seth and listening to his imaginative stories. He was the best storyteller Everett had ever heard. They were always Bible stories. But the way Seth told them, it was as if he'd never heard them before.

They got to know the dogs well and played with them. Eagerly both dogs obeyed their commands. Tina especially was good with them. She even taught them a trick: to lie down, then jump up on command and grab a ball out of her outstretched hand. Just like the dolphins at Sea World, Everett thought. Seth was delighted. He said, "Anytime I'm not here and you come by, feel free to unlatch Bump and Whip and play. You're all good kids. I trust you."

They practiced with their slingshots in the woods and

D.G. made one each for Tina and Linc. Soon, they could sling stones accurately at twenty feet. Everett could hit a tree at twenty paces eight out of ten times now. He wasn't as good as D.G. But he was getting it. Better and better.

One Sunday afternoon, though, it was quiet and Everett lay out on his front lawn sunbathing. He was in the middle of cutting it and had decided to take a rest. Chuck and Stuart walked by and Chuck called out. "Hey, Abels! How's your friend, Scarface? Still playing with the retard?"

Everett sat up immediately, feeling angry and defensive. "Shut up, Chuck. There's nothing wrong with D.G. And he's not a retard."

Chuck gave him a long, superior look, then said, "Well, I have something for you to do. We're going fishing next Saturday—you know, my gramp's place in the pineys—" They had gone several times the previous summer, and Everett knew it was a good time. "I thought maybe you'd like to go. So I decided to make you an offer. You want to hear it?"

Everett eyed Chuck. That was him. Deals. He'd never thought about it before, but now he remembered how Chuck would con him and Stuart into running errands and doing odd jobs for him by cutting a little deal.

"I don't know, Chuck. I might be busy." He was interested in hearing what Chuck wanted, even though he knew he probably wouldn't go.

"Get me one of Scarface's little notebooks. Any one.

You do that and you're in. Got it?"

Everett snorted. "Get out of here, Chuck. I'm not interested."

Chuck gazed at him evenly, smiling his crafty smile. "You'll come around. You always do."

Anger burned through Everett's gut, and he stood, clenching his fist. "Drop dead, Chuck!"

The bigger boy leaned forward with a sneer, sticking his chin out. "Go ahead, let me see your stuff. Just like with O'Brien."

Everett's face suddenly felt hot and he turned, picked up his glass and shirt and started walking to the house.

"Retard lover!" Chuck called as Everett stomped into the garage.

With an angry yell, he balled up his shirt and hurled it at the door. "He's such a jerk!" he yelled.

But inside the old fear twitched and sputtered. *Yellow belly. Chicken! That's all you are!*

19
Cigarettes

In mid-July, Tina and Linc's dad finally filled their pool, and the group enjoyed swimming and playing games in it. Mr. Watterson bought several one-person boats made out of green plastic, and D.G. led them all in water battles and races. They were great for sunning and floating around in them half asleep.

Then one Wednesday morning, the foursome gathered on the street corner talking about a new music group. The weather was hot and sticky, but no one wanted to swim. Suddenly, Chuck and Stuart came around the corner, and spotted them. They swaggered over to the group, trying to act tough and mean. "I suppose you guys are the ones who put up the rope swing down by Rocky Creek."

"We did," D.G. immediately answered, not flustered. "You can just leave it alone."

Chuck smiled. "Yeah, well don't be surprised."

"About what?" D.G. said.

"Just surprised," Chuck said with a crafty smile.

Everett wanted to walk away. He said to D.G., "Let's just go."

But when they turned, Chuck and Stuart followed them. Stuart pulled at Chuck's arm, telling him to forget it, but Chuck shook him off. "Just thought we might like to come with you all," he said.

"What?" Everett said. Alarm signals rang in his mind.

Chuck shrugged. "It's not like we don't live in the same neighborhood."

Wavering between thinking it could be a trap and the desire to be friends again, Everett turned to D.G. "Let's take them back in the woods. Maybe we can introduce them to Bump and Whip. See how they like them."

Tina didn't like the idea. But D.G. raised his eyebrows. "Yeah, let's."

Everyone quickly agreed, and they all went down to the rope swing and swung across. No one said much. But in the woods, Chuck kept cutting up, nearly insulting D.G. several times. When they passed the road to the run-down house, Chuck mentioned it to Stuart, and Everett said they'd already been inside and seen everything.

"Did you find anything interesting?" Chuck asked.

"Not really," Everett answered. It seemed almost like old times.

When they reached Seth's house, the truck was gone out of the driveway, as Everett expected. Still, Tina unlatched Bump and Whip. The two dogs pranced around them, licking hands, and giving Chuck and Stuart friendly sniffs.

Linc and Tina showed the two outsiders some of the dogs' tricks. But Chuck wasn't impressed. "Any dog can retrieve a stick," he said.

After standing around for a few more minutes, D.G. said they all ought to explore more in the woods, maybe go down the creek. They left the dogs tied up back at the house and headed up the road. Everett knew D.G. probably had some cupcakes in his backpack, but he wasn't sure whether D.G. would care to share them with Chuck and Stuart.

As D.G. tried to get Stuart talking about sports and the Philadelphia Phillies, Everett listened. But Stuart wouldn't talk. Chuck began making sarcastic remarks. Everett sensed it really was impossible that they all be friends. Then as they stood in the middle of the road discussing what to do, suddenly Chuck said, "Maybe each of us can tell something no one knows about us."

Instantly, Everett knew Chuck was up to something.

Before anyone could protest, Chuck turned to Tina, "You have any secrets you'd like to tell?"

"Not to you," she said, folding her arms and returning his stare without flinching.

"What about you, D.G., or whatever your name is?"

D.G. glanced at Everett. "I don't want to play that kind of game. Let's go down the creek."

Chuck didn't move. "Well, I know one about Everett," he said with a sly grin. Before anyone could stop him, he began telling the story of the fight with O'Brien. Though D.G. interrupted and Tina and Linc told him they didn't want to hear about it, Everett didn't try to stop him. He bowed his head, but he could feel Tina's eyes looking from him to Chuck. When Chuck was done, he said, "So what do you think of that?"

"I already knew all about it." D.G. said flatly and set his chin with anger flashing in his eyes.

Chuck turned to Tina and Linc. "And you?"

"I know Everett's no coward, or yellow belly as you call him," Tina said. "I'd go with him anytime."

Linc nodded. "Why don't you just leave?"

Relieved, Everett looked up into Chuck's cold blue eyes. The big boy's face clouded. "Oh, we'll see who are the real cowards around here." He pulled a pack of cigarettes out of his pocket. "I thought we were going to see if you yellow bellies have any guts. Well, here's your chance."

Everett's heart began pounding. His mom and dad would never let him smoke a cigarette, not at eleven years old, anyway. But Chuck lit the cigarette and sucked on it, then passed it to Stuart. Stuart took a long drag and blew it out noisily. Tina folded her arms. "I suppose that proves you are two big, brave boys."

Chuck snapped the cigarette from Stuart and held it out to Tina. "Okay, show us if you do anything besides play with your Barbies."

Wrinkling her nose, Tina shook her head with irritation. "I don't smoke cigarettes. It's disgusting. It doesn't prove anything except that you two are idiots."

Stiffening, Chuck sneered and turned to D.G. "How about you, Scarface? You're tough, aren't you?"

D.G. glared at him. "Smoking a cigarette is dumb. Real dumb. I thought you had more brains than that."

Passing over Linc, Chuck turned to Everett. "Well, here's your big chance, Mr. Yellow Streak. Let's see what you can do with this." He took a drag and held it out to Everett. D.G., Tina, and Linc were all staring at him, but Everett couldn't read in their faces what they were thinking.

Everett swallowed. What would it prove? A rising string of smoke stung his nostrils as Chuck held the cigarette just under Everett's nose. He flinched, wrinkling his nose.

"See, you can't even take a little smoke!"

Without thinking about it, Everett suddenly snatched the cigarette out of Chuck's hand, then threw it to the ground, stomping it out. "Lay off, Chuck. We're not smoking your stupid cigarette."

Chuck's face darkened and he stepped forward, no more than a foot from Everett's face. He exhaled the remaining smoke into his eyes. "Still a yellow belly, huh? You're about as tough as . . ." He gave Everett a little shove.

Falling back, Everett yelled, "You don't need to act like this, Chuck." He didn't want to fight. Not because he knew Chuck could take him, but because he didn't want to involve the others. Chuck was his problem.

"Yeah, still a yellow belly. And a jerk. Now add to that the fact that you play with Barbies."

"Lay off, Chuck. I'm not . . ."

"Prove it!"

Chuck shoved him again.

Waving a skinny fist, Tina stepped forward. "Why don't you just leave, you big jerk!"

D.G. and Linc moved closer, their fists at their sides, ready. Stuart looked from Chuck to the others and started to say something, but Chuck shook off Tina. "You even need a girl to protect you, yellow belly." He spat on the ground to his side. "What a wimp!"

He turned to go, then suddenly whipped around. "You want to prove you're not a yellow belly, Abels? You want to prove it? Then you know what to do." He glanced at D.G. Instantly, Everett knew what he was referring to: D.G.'s diary. "Meet me at the house up that road there tomorrow at three o'clock with the goods and I'll call it square. Otherwise . . ." He snorted and spat into the dirt.

Everett stood his ground. "Get out of here! I'm not doing anything . . ."

Screwing up his face with disgust, Chuck stepped

forward, only inches from Everett's face. Then he spat into it.

The flecks of spit seared on his cheeks and nose like burning bits of steel.

Chuck's mouth curled into a sneering smile. "Yeah. Yellow. That's what you are. Just stand there and take it, or run like you always did." He turned and stalked toward the path toward the woods. "Come on, Stuart, let's get out of here."

Everett's cheek twitched. His face was wet from the spit. His heart banged wildly in his chest. He couldn't move. He couldn't look up at any of the others. The only sound was of Stuart and Chuck walking off toward the woods. No one spoke.

When Chuck reached the trees, he turned just before ducking down the path. He shouted, "Three o'clock, Abels. Remember that, yellow belly! Three o'clock!"

Everett blinked. No one looked at him. He knew exactly what they were thinking. *Yellow belly!* After another few seconds of silence, he slowly wiped the spit off his face.

When they were gone, D.G. seethed, "Why didn't you smash the jerk? We would have helped you."

Everett's lip quivered. Tina touched his shoulder. "It's all right. Something's wrong with that kid."

But it was true. He should've hit Chuck. Even if it meant being flattened. He was a coward. He was a yellow, chicken-hearted wimp, and there was only one way to prove he wasn't.

"Come on," D.G. said. "Forget that guy. We don't need him around."

Everett said nothing. Everyone began plodding quietly toward the woods. No one said a word. D.G. and Tina kept looking back at Everett, but he couldn't meet their eyes.

Then he heard D.G. saying, "Why don't we all go back to my house? My mom has lots of stuff to eat and we can play Monopoly or something."

"All right!" said Linc, trying to generate some enthusiasm.

Tina turned to look at Everett. "Will you come too?"

He shrugged, staring off into the woods. "Yeah, I guess so."

When they reached the rope, it was dangling into the stream. Chuck and Stuart hadn't even had the courtesy to tie it up. Without a complaint, D.G. crossed through the water, then sent the rope back to the others.

As Everett watched, he realized he was shaking. All he could think was that somehow he had to prove to himself he wasn't a coward.

20
The Diary

Mrs. Frankl told them they had to be quiet because Mr. Frankl was home taking a nap that afternoon, but D.G. said not to worry about it. He slept like "the bottom of the ocean." Tina giggled at the expression.

The four filed into D.G.'s room and he pulled down the Monopoly game. Everett pretended to watch, but he stole a glance at the notebooks on the second shelf. There were about ten of them. The thought occurred to him, *D.G. wouldn't notice if you just took it for a few hours.*

He pushed the thought away. He would never do that! Let Chuck call him what he wanted, but he wouldn't betray D.G.

Linc and Tina laid out the game and everyone chose one of the small metal figurines used as playing pieces. D.G. handed out the money and asked Everett to be the bank.

The thought hammered away inside him: *Just borrow it. You don't even have to look at it. Not even let Chuck look at it. Just show him you did it. D.G. would even want you to do it. To prove you're not . . .*

When Everett flinched, Tina touched his arm. "Are you all right?"

He nodded absently, his vision blurring. He felt as though his mind was filled with muck. "I don't feel so good."

"I'll get some pretzels and drinks," D.G. said, jumping up.

Tina and Linc kept glancing at Everett. Linc started to say something twice, but he stopped before saying anything.

Trying to squelch the hideous thoughts, Everett suddenly heard the word shriek in his brain like a curse: *Yellow belly!* He swallowed, trying to catch his breath.

D.G. came back with the drinks and a bag of pretzels. Linc and he devoured several. Everett could feel their eyes on him as he crunched one in his teeth. But it tasted like grit in his mouth, and he had to force himself to eat the whole thing.

Just take the notebook. No one will know. Just take the notebook when they're all gone.

Everett squeezed his eyes shut. *No*, he shouted in his mind. *I can't do that.*

The game began. Everett played mechanically.

Everyone bought up properties and soon they were all absorbed in the game. But Everett's mind roared with the words, *Yellow belly! Coward! Wimp!* D.G. said, "Why does Davis have to be so mean? I think we should just fight him or something. Even if we lose, at least we tried."

Everyone glanced worriedly at Everett, but he didn't say anything.

Tina said, "He's got something wrong in his head, that's what I say. I wouldn't give him a crumb of one of D.G.'s cupcakes."

Linc and D.G. chuckled. "I don't know," D.G. said, "maybe that's what he needs. One with arsenic in it."

Again they laughed, but it was a nervous, uneasy laugh.

"I just think we should all meet him tomorrow at three and tell him to soak his head," D.G. said. "If he wants a fight, then let's fight him."

"There has to be a better way," Tina replied with her jaw set. "I don't think fighting is the way to settle problems."

D.G. nodded reluctantly. "Yeah, I guess you're right." He glanced at Everett again. Everett felt D.G.'s deep brown eyes on him a moment, then turning away.

The game went on. D.G., Linc, and Tina talked quietly, trying to include Everett in their conversation. But his mind was far off. He moved almost without thinking. An argument arose in his mind.

Just take it. Just for a few hours. D.G.'ll never notice. He'd want you to, anyway.

Yellow belly!

You could put it in your backpack and no one would know.

Retard lover. Jerk.

Everett was sweating now, and he had a headache. He kept swallowing and glancing around the room, but it looked fuzzy. He felt as though the walls were closing in on him. He had to do something. He had to get out. *That's right, run. Like you always do. Run! Run! RUN!*

A sickening feeling came over him. Then he heard D.G. say, "Your move, Everett."

He tried to hold himself in place, to be natural, to get the burning out of his eyes and his chest.

Suddenly Linc said, "I'm going to the bathroom."

"Yeah, me, too," Tina said. "I guess twins even have to go at the same time."

D.G. laughed. "We have two bathrooms. Come on. I'll show you."

A moment later, the room was empty except for Everett. He sat on the floor. His backpack lay on the bed. Only an arm's length away was the diary. *All you have to take is one. Now's your chance. Do it.*

Yellow belly. Yellow belly! YELLOW BELLY!

Instantly, Everett was on his feet. He rushed to the door, listened for any sounds, then gulped and skirted around the bed to the shelves. With a blink and a terrified sigh, he picked up the second-to-last book on the shelf. He stared at the cover. "Book twelve, April 1 to July 1. Dodai Gamaliel Frankl. Personal Diary."

Everett swallowed. *Maybe I should open it, just look at it.*

He started to open the book, but something inside him knew it was all wrong. He couldn't do it. It was like the thing was sacred or something. It was a betrayal of the worst sort.

He heard voices down the hall. He stared at the backpack and then at the shelf. It would only take a second to put it into the backpack.

But it's wrong! In a moment, Everett realized the truth. He carefully placed the book back on the shelf and breathed out quietly. *At least*, he thought, *I've done one right thing.*

Seconds later, D.G. raced in with Tina trying to tickle him. The instant he saw Everett on the bed he stopped and stared.

"What are you doing?" D.G.'s voice had a sudden fright and tightness in it that Everett had never heard before.

With a weary sigh, Everett swiveled around. He thought of lying, but he knew he should simply tell them. The truth. That was about the only thing he had on his side.

D.G. hurried over toward the bookshelf, staring at Everett. "Are you okay? Your face is white."

Everett nodded. Linc walked in. Everett cleared his throat. "D.G., remember when Chuck said today to meet him at the house?"

D.G. nodded. "Yeah, I think we all ought to go. Teach that guy a lesson."

Swallowing, Everett sighed noisily. "Well, the reason he

wants to meet me there . . ." He noticed his heart was louder than his voice. "Is because he wants me to bring one of the books—one of the books in your diary."

D.G.'s eyes popped a moment. "And you were just looking at them now?"

His eyes tearing, Everett hung his head. "I'm sorry. I almost took one. "But I know it was wrong."

The room was dead quiet. Everett shook his head. His eyes burned. "I'm really sorry," he said. He could barely look up. But he had to meet D.G.'s eyes. Everett's dad always said that. Just look them in the eye.

Instantly, D.G. beamed his crinkly grin. He had that triumphant look in his eyes that always made Everett feel more confident. But somehow now he just felt shame.

D.G pulled one of the diaries out. "Would you like me to read you all something from it?" He looked from Everett to Tina to Linc.

Everett immediately shook his head. "You don't have to, D.G. They're your private thoughts."

"No, I want to," D.G. said. "Who knows who might ever read it? And I'm not ashamed of it or anything. Sometimes I'm really protective. But let me read you something." He opened up to a page. Then he said,

"Oh, this is about the time Seth told us the story of David and Goliath." He began reading, " 'It was a great story. I never heard anyone as good as Seth. He's a master. I hope one day I can tell stories like him.

"What was even better was that he knows about David

and Jonathan. That's how I feel with Everett and Linc and Tina. They're my best friends. I hope our friendship never ends." He looked up brightly.

Everett's throat hardened into a lump. How could he almost have betrayed this guy? He glanced at Tina and Linc, and they were both very quiet.

"Do you want me to read some more?"

"Not now," said Tina. "I think we have to help Everett."

D.G. gazed at Everett thoughtfully. "All right. Chuck Davis wants my diary. Let's give him one!"

Everyone gasped. Everett said, "But we can't do that. He'd chew you up."

"No," D.G. said. "Not one of my real ones. I'd never share them with anyone but you guys. No, we'll make one up. I have extra notebooks, empty ones. We'll make up something real special for Chuck Davis and Stuart Coble. You know what I mean?" D.G. looked craftily from Everett to Tina to Linc. "We'll write up some real blasters for them both, okay?" Feeling the shame and guilt disappear, Everett suddenly smiled. "I think I get what you mean."

Tina laughed. "You mean like the joke's on him."

"Right," D.G. said, "Look, maybe all of you can come over after dinner, and then we have tomorrow morning, too. We can think up all kinds of jokes and things we can do to put into it. Really get him."

Now Tina and Linc were chuckling happily. "I'm going to love to see his face when he sees this," Tina said.

"No!" D.G. said, shaking his head emphatically.

"Everett'll have to do it like I don't know about it. Because then Chuck will suspect. We have to make him think it's the real thing. But first, since you know him, Everett, we have to think of every embarrassing moment in Chuck's life that you know about. Every one."

Everett smiled. "Oh, believe me, I know plenty. Him striking out several times in tight Little League games and then trying to blame it on someone else on the team. The time he lied to the teacher about a project that Stuart and I did for him. I know a lot of things." For a moment, he felt very strong and sure. But something in the back of his mind struggled. *Is that right, is that the right way to deal with it?* But he pushed the thought away.

They went downstairs. "Come over after dinner," D.G. said. "We'll cook this one up hot."

21
The Trap

That night, the foursome dreamed up every joke, story, and embarrassment they could think of and wrote it into the book. Everett dredged up numerous secret events and situations he and Chuck and Stuart had been in that would humiliate Chuck if anyone knew. In the end, they filled about twenty pages of funny jabs to Chuck's pride. When Chuck read this, D.G. was sure he'd not only hit the roof, he'd go through it.

The book started: "The adventures of Chuckie the Chump and his faithful servant, Stu the Hoo." They began with a a crazy, rhyming poem about Chuckie's tendency to lie, steal, and bully only to be bested by the "Fearsome Foursome."

Everett wrote that "Chuckie was unluckie and got stuckie in muckie." He explained to the other three, "Chuck, Stuart and I were hiking around a farmhouse at the end of the street, and Chuck got stuck in some mud. He was so scared, he screamed he was in quicksand. But when we pulled him out, it was only a pigsty. Chuck made us swear we'd never tell."

It was great fun and when they were finished, Everett was more than satisfied that the final laugh would be on Chuck. He did feel a little uneasy that they weren't treating Chuck as they'd like to be treated. But he knew it was only in fun, and no one else would see the book.

Together they came up with a plan. Everett had to go in alone. If Chuck started a fight, he'd just have to fight back. Everett decided he wasn't going through the rest of his life being afraid of Chuck Davis.

D.G. said to everyone, "We all go to the house, but Everett goes inside first." He turned to Everett, "You get Chuck upstairs, then read to him a few passages from the book right by the window in the upper right side room. If Chuck tries to attack you, throw the book out the window to the ground where we'll be standing. But if Chuck promises to lay off us, we'll all burn it together, and no one will ever know about it."

They worked on the book for several hours. In the end, they were satisfied that it would put Chuck in his place and force him to stop needling Everett.

From D.G.'s house, Everett called Chuck to make sure he'd be there the next day. Mrs. Davis answered and said, "Oh, hi, Everett. Haven't seen you around for a while. You want to speak to Chuck?"

A minute later, Chuck was on the phone. "Yeah?"

Everett hesitated, then said, "I'll meet you at the house at three o'clock tomorrow. Okay?"

"Oh, it's the yellow belly. You have the goods?"

"Yeah."

"Great! Just think, after tomorrow, you and I will be back together like never before." Everett recognized the sarcasm in his voice.

It made him feel angry and all the more right about the book, even though he suspected they should probably forget the whole joke.

"Yeah, right," Everett said and hung up quickly, then sighed wearily. "I guess it's a 'go.' "

D.G. cheered and Linc danced a little jig. But Everett noticed a quiet reserve in Tina that he also felt.

That night before bed his mother visited his room and sat down next to him on the bed. After some talk, he asked, "Mom, do you think God ever gives a person a second chance?"

"At what, honey?" Her deep gray eyes were sympathetic, but he knew she had no idea what had happened.

"Anything. Like when you've made a bad mistake?"

She nodded and smiled with calm assurance. "Of course, Evvie. You know what it says in Romans. He 'makes all things to work together for good to those that love Him.' You can be sure if you love Him, He'll work everything for good."

"But how?"

She gazed at him thoughtfully. "You're talking about the problem with Chuck again?"

"Sort of."

"I don't know how or what God will do," she said with a sigh. "But already I think you can see He's done some good. You have three very nice new friends."

He hadn't thought of that. "Yeah, I guess so."

She squeezed his shoulder.

"Mom?"

She looked at him again, waiting.

"Do you think it's right to hurt someone deliberately?"

She didn't answer for a long time. "You're not planning to hurt someone, are you?"

He shifted uneasily on the bed. "I don't know. I don't think we could hurt this someone."

She took his hand and patted it. "Do what's right, Evvie. Just do what's right. God will work it out."

"Yeah, I guess so."

After she went out, he lay in bed thinking about the plan. He told himself it was just a joke. No one would be hurt, much less Chuck. He'd probably laugh it off as the feeble attempt of a jerk to get back at him. But Everett wasn't sure.

He finally fell asleep to jittery dreams.

It was past three o'clock when they reached the clearing to the abandoned house. D.G. strutted down the road, singing a song while Linc and Tina walked on either side of Everett, speaking words of encouragement. Both D.G. and Everett wore their backpacks. Everett concealed the diary in his.

They reached the clearing. D.G., Linc, and Tina waited in the woods while Everett proceeded toward the house alone. "We'll give you five minutes," D.G. whispered as Everett crossed the open lawn..

Everett was in no hurry, but as he peeked inside the front door, Chuck called from the top of the stairs. "You got it, yellow belly?" Stuart positioned himself behind Chuck, grinning and snickering.

Any guilt Everett felt about the book immediately disappeared. Chuck was a nasty guy. He had to be put in his place.

Everett called from the bottom of the stairs, "Let me come up. I want to talk to you." When Chuck motioned to him, he climbed up, praying that nothing would go wrong.

When he reached the top, Chuck blocked the way. "Where's the book, jerko?"

Everett pushed past him into the room. "Just wait a minute. Let's go into the room here. You want to see it, just do what I say."

Chuck squinted suspiciously, then said to Stuart, "Okay, we'll give him one minute to play his little game."

Trying to be casual, Everett walked over to the window and leaned against it. "I think you'll be surprised what's in D.G.'s diary." He pulled it out of his backpack.

"Yeah," Chuck sneered. "What could the little creep write that would surprise me? He probably writes nice little poems about his grandmother. But it will make good reading to my friends."

"Oh, you're going to read it to all your friends?"

Chuck's lip twisted. "Just give me the thing." He stepped forward menacingly.

"Wait a minute," Everett said, swallowing back the fear. "You come any closer and it goes out the window." He waved the book toward the opening.

Chuck hesitated, then looked behind him. "So what? I can beat you down the stairs."

"No, some people are out there who will grab it if I throw it out."

"Who? Your jerky friends?"

"Just people."

Chuck stepped closer, his face flushed with anger. "Give me the thing or I cream you one."

"I want to read a little to you, all right?" Everett's face felt hot, and he was already sweating through his shirt. His throat felt dry as summer sand.

Folding his arms, Chuck snorted, "Oh, so this is story time? All right. I can get into that." He grinned at Stuart. "Let's see what the little retard says."

Everett cleared his throat. "Page one. 'This is my story.

In it I will reveal my deepest thoughts and longings, my heartfelt feelings, the girls I have secretly wanted to like me, and the battles I have engaged in, won, and lost.' "

Chuck grinned with jubilation. "So the guy's flowery." He smiled at Stuart. "This will make a really good joke in sixth grade—'Bring in your favorite story'— you know?"

Ignoring him, Everett read on. " 'I will tell you of my greatest triumphs and also my most humiliating defeats. Perhaps one day this diary will be published, and I would not want to paint my life as a lie. And so, we must get on now with the story of Chuckie the Chump and Stu the Hoo.' "

Flinching with surprise, Chuck glared at Everett. "What?"

Everett hurried on. " 'In it I tell about the time Chuck got caught in Farmer Lewis's pigsty . . .' "

Chuck stepped forward.

The book quivered in Everett's hand, but he said hotly, "You come any closer, and the book goes out the window, Chuck." He read on, " 'I'll tell you about how Chuck kept a picture of Jennifer Shulmann on his dresser for a year . . .' "

"What?" Chuck roared. "What is this?"

Holding the book out over the window, Everett hissed, "Any closer and down it goes."

"What is this book?"

Everett said in hard-etched words, "It's every secret you never wanted anyone to know about, and it'll be given, one by one, to every kid in our sixth-grade class before school begins if . . ."

Chuck clenched his fist. "What is this, blackmail?"

"You lay off, Chuck, and we'll all gladly burn this book in D.G.'s backyard. But you keep acting like a jerk about all this . . ."

Advancing with fists pulled up, Chuck shouted, "I suppose you told them everything?"

"Everything I could remember." Everett breathed more evenly now that it was out.

Chuck turned to Stuart. "Run downstairs and get outside the window. Hurry!"

Stuart scurried out.

Turning back to Everett, Chuck intoned, "Now what are you going to do, jerko?"

Everett glanced out the window. He noticed for the first time that it was nailed shut. Even with the panes gone, leaving jagged edges, he couldn't just jump out or even slide through. He remembered then that all the windows on this floor were nailed shut.

He still didn't see D.G. or Linc and Tina. Suddenly he realized how afraid he was of Chuck. He knew Chuck could probably beat him to a tar. But his fear was of another nature. He made Everett feel little, as if he didn't matter, as if he was nothing. That was what Everett hated most. He'd never been able to defend against it. Until now, with D.G., Linc, and Tina.

Hardening his jaw, Everett said, "You want to fight, Chuck, is that it?"

"Yeah, I wouldn't mind beating your little brain in. But

first I want that book." He quickly slid to the other side of the window. "I want that book, Abels."

Everett held it out over the window. Then he heard a scuffle below. "Don't throw it down Everett, Stuart's here," D.G. cried.

At the same instant, Chuck leapt at Everett and straight-armed him in the chest. The book clattered to the floor. Everett bent over, his breath gone, clutching his rib cage. Chuck crouched down to pick up the book, eyeing Everett furiously.

As he rested, Everett caught a breath. Forming a plan, he suddenly leapt at the bigger boy, trying to tackle him. He hit Chuck full front, but then he threw Everett off, smacking him on the side of the head. Everett rolled over and started to rise, but Chuck lashed out with his foot, catching Everett in the stomach. It felt as though his insides caught fire.

Everett rolled against the wall and slumped down against it, trying to protect his gut with his hands. He tried again to get to his feet, but Chuck pounced on him. "Boy, am I going to enjoy this!"

Cursing, Chuck lifted Everett with an uppercut, then whammed him back into the wall. Blood ran down Everett's chin. He felt dizzy and tried to get his balance against the wall. But Chuck bent down again, grabbing his jaw. "Man, I just want to see you bleed, Abels."

He pulled his arm back, ready to slam Everett's nose. But Everett threw a wild jab that glanced off Chuck's chin.

Pivoting and throwing Everett off, Chuck laughed and drew back again. Everett prepared to try to dodge the blow. He briefly caught Chuck's eye. For the first time he saw the hatred there like fire.

Then he heard a cry on the stairs. "Someone is coming!" It was Stuart's voice. Chuck spun around, for the moment forgetting what he wanted to do.

Seconds later, Stuart, D.G., Linc, and Tina ran into the room. "We had to come in through the back door," Stuart cried, out of breath.

Chuck stepped back from Everett, grabbing the book. Everett pushed himself up. Pain jabbed his side. He sucked at his lip to stop the blood.

"Somebody just pulled into the yard," Stuart repeated. "Somebody in a station wagon. I think there's three of them. And one of them looked like John O'Brien."

D.G. and Tina ran over to Everett, taking his hand and helping him up. "You okay?" D.G. said, looking into his face. Everett nodded. Tina pulled out a handkerchief and dabbed at his lip. D.G. was clearly fuming.

Chuck ran to the window and looked down.

A moment later, Everett heard a man's voice, "Let's get this done quickly."

"Right," another man's voice said. "Come on, Johnny, let's check the cellar, make sure everything's there."

This time we're really in for it, Everett thought as the salty taste of blood stung his tongue.

22
Thieves

Chuck pointed his finger at Everett and started to say something, but it was obvious he was afraid. Stuart pulled at his arm. "We gotta go, man. You know what O'Brien said last time."

His face white, Chuck nodded with barely controlled anger. "This isn't over, Abels," he said. But the air obviously had gone out of him. He started out of the room toward the stairs.

D.G. ran over to the window and looked out, then muttered something Everett couldn't understand. Chuck turned in the doorway and said low and quiet, "He'll beat the tar out of us this time, Stuart. What are we going to do?"

Stuart looked at Chuck helplessly as Linc whispered from the stairs, "Shut up! They're coming into the house."

They could hear the voices of the men as they came in. "I say we get it, sell it all, then forget this place," said one voice.

"We can't, Jack," said the second. "It's the only place we got to hide it."

A third voice said, "Do you want me to take the tape decks out first?"

"That's O'Brien," D.G. whispered. "That older guy must be his big brother. I've seen them together at the shopping center."

The six kids crouched against the wall at the top of the stairs, out of sight.

"Yeah, I'll open up the cellar," the one named Jack said.

Inching over to the opening to the stairs, D.G. put his finger to his lips. "They must be selling the stuff that was in the boxes downstairs to some illegal operation."

The three thieves noisily clumped around downstairs. Everett knew instantly that was what it was all about. The theft ring. What his father had talked about. O'Brien hung around the shopping center keeping an eye on the trucks so his brother could steal the stereo equipment. They probably stored it in the cellar.

Everett wiped his mouth. The blood lay wet and red on the back of his hand.

He heard the one named Jack say, "You open it up, Dan. I'll look out back. Maybe we can smoke up some of that dope."

One of them worked on the padlock to the door into the basement. Another turned on a boom box and played a heavy metal tape Everett didn't recognize. It was loud enough to give the group a chance to breathe more easily and not worry about making noise.

"They must be hiding it down there," said D.G. He walked quietly to the room where the newspapers lay on the floor, then held up an article about electronics thieves. "This is them!"

Chuck snatched the article out of his hand and read it. It was about a local ring of truck thieves who ransacked trucks at local shopping centers.

"I don't believe this," Chuck said.

"Just be quiet," Tina whispered angrily.

"But we've got to do something," said D.G.

"Like what?" said Tina. "Go down and say, 'Hi, we're here!' "

Chuck eyed everyone. "Stuart and I will just run for it. I don't give diddly about the rest of you."

D.G. shook his head. "You won't make it. If they see you, they won't stop. They know you'll call the police."

"I'll make a deal."

"Yeah, but remember what O'Brien said," Stuart added. "He'd love to get you like this."

Chuck swore. "What are we going to do?"

"We?" D.G. said, eyeing him resentfully. "So it's 'we' now?"

Chuck glanced around apprehensively at everyone. "All right, so we had a little fight. I have the book now, no harm done. Let's just get out of here."

Everett sensed, though, whatever chance Chuck got he'd take and hang the rest of them.

Chuck gripped the notebook in his right hand. Tina glared at him with contempt, but Everett recognized the fear in his eyes. For the moment, it stirred him. Maybe Chuck wasn't so brave after all.

"We have to get out and get the police," said D.G. "We've got to stop them before they have a chance to dispose of the evidence." He tiptoed back into the room and studied the nailed windows. Then he said, "All the windows are nailed shut and the nails are big. We couldn't get them out, not without a hammer."

Everett glanced up at the hole in the ceiling. "Maybe we can get out through the attic. We could go out the side window and down the pipe. The window's big enough and it doesn't have any glass or screen."

D.G. stared at the hole. "Not a bad idea."

Chuck started to speak, but Tina cut him off. "I think it'll work."

"Then let's go," Everett said. "We don't know how long they'll be here, and who knows what they'll do if they catch us."

They listened to the three thieves move around

downstairs. Linc kept a lookout, but there was always someone in the hall or front to prevent their escape. The music blared loudly. Then they heard Jack say, "You're sure none of your friends know about this place, Johnny?"

"I haven't told them. I swear, Jack."

"Well, you better not. We find any around here, we'll have to deal with them tough. Because if the cops ever find out about this, we're dead. You got it?"

"Yeah. I swear, Jack."

Everett grabbed D.G.'s arm. "I say we get going. We can get out, and we'd better do it now."

D.G.'s eyes darted about with indecision, but finally he nodded. "Okay, you're the best climber, Everett. You go first. Then Tina, because she's . . ." Tina gave him a tough look in return, but Everett knew what D.G. was thinking. "Because she should go next," he said.

Someone turned the boom box down a little, but it was still loud enough to drown out any noise the group upstairs might make. Some smoke drifted up the stairs. It had a sweet, rancid odor.

D.G. whispered, "I bet it's cocaine or something."

He moved back from the stairwell and gathered the group. "Okay, now's our chance. We'll all go out through the roof. Everett, get ready."

"Just don't run out on us," Chuck said with a snicker.

Instantly, Tina answered with quiet anger. "Look, I've about had it with your stuff. Just because you're bigger . . ." She bunched her fist, but then she said, "If you have any better ideas, then say them. Otherwise, shut up. You're not so smart."

Chuck started to make a remark, then sank back into silence.

Everett began working out a plan in his mind. The rock music below gave them a chance to talk a little louder. "Give me your belts," he said. "I'll make a rope out of them. Then give me a hoist up. I'll grab the upper edge and pull myself in. Then I'll let down the belts and help pull you up."

"Thinking just like an Israeli commando," D.G. said with a grin. But Everett worried that the thieves would still catch them. They had to move fast.

Everett crept out into the hall, keeping low. The three thieves sat on the stoop, smoking their drugs, and talking. It was midafternoon. Sweat dripped off Everett's nose. He could see that even if the thieves turned around, they probably wouldn't see them unless they looked directly up the stairs.

"Let's be real careful," D.G. said. "Think like Israelis."

Everett, Linc, and D.G. took their belts off. But Chuck refused, and then Stuart did. Chuck said to Everett, "Just don't run, yellow belly."

Everett suddenly realized Chuck wasn't going to help them at all. He had been watching the stairs for a chance to run. Everett knew he had to work even faster. Chuck wouldn't flinch at betraying any of them.

Everett hooked the belts together, then wrapped them

around his waist. D.G. and Linc made a step with their hands linked together.

It was like a missile shot. Everett grabbed the inside of the rim of the hatch and pulled up into it soundlessly. He wriggled through the hole and groped his way inside, then unlatched the belts. The attic smelled musty and stifling. The air there was even hotter, and he could barely breathe. But the window at the far end loomed open and inviting, like a break in a storm. They could escape if they were fast.

The floor was ribbed with two-by-fours, about sixteen inches apart. They'd have to be careful not to step between them. The ceiling was just Sheetrock.

He lowered the belt rope down through the hole. Moments later, he hoisted Tina silently through the hole.

"That was easy," she said.

"Yeah," said Everett. "Now the hard part."

He was about to feed the belts back down, when he heard a shout.

"Hey!"

Everett jumped, then he looked down through the hole and saw D.G. and Linc spin around. They threw their arms up. "It's okay. Just us," cried D.G.

Everett heard boots on the stairs.

"Who are you?" an angry voice said.

Something inside Everett's mind seemed to burst. Now they were really into it.

23
The Hole in the Wall

Everett barely dared to breathe. He moved back from the hole and motioned to Tina to do the same. A black, strangling terror filled him. He heard Jack say below, "What are you doing here, kid?"

"We were exploring," said D.G.

There was a scuffle and Linc yelled, "Hey, that hurts."

Then little O'Brien said, "I know these guys. I beat them up awhile ago with Mullen." O'Brien began taunting Chuck and Stuart. "What's that in your hand, Davis?" O'Brien snatched the notebook out of Chuck's hand. Jack pinned D.G.'s arm around his back. D.G. cried, "You're going to break my arm."

"It'll hurt a lot worse than this, kid, if you don't do what we say."

Everett heard Chuck say, "I've got a little secret for you."

Instantly, Everett knew Chuck intended to tell the thieves where they were. He had to move. Get out. Fast. He signaled to Tina to start scrambling toward the window. Then he heard Jack say, "Shut up, kid!"

Chuck answered, "But I have . . ."

"Shut up! Another word and I punch your lights out."

The thieves began talking among themselves. Fortunately, the boom box made enough noise to cover any creaks Everett and Tina were making by crossing the attic. They moved like spiders along the two-by-fours. When they stopped at the window, Everett could see Tina's lip trembling.

"What are we going to do, Everett?"

He knew he had to be calm, to think. He flashed her a quick smile and grabbed her hand. "It'll be okay." But inside his mind he was screaming, *What am I going to do?*

Tina looked as though she might cry, but she seemed to take courage in Everett's confidence. "Okay, we just have to help them and not get caught."

At least the thieves didn't know about them, Everett figured. He turned to look out the window. The belts were bunched up in his hand.

Tina waited motionless behind him. Then a new idea hit him. "Seth!" he whispered. "We've got to get to Seth." He peeked out the window. He heard the thieves still arguing in the hallway.

He knew they had to go now, while O'Brian and his friends were all upstairs. That was their only chance of getting to Seth and rescuing D.G. and Linc and the others. Didn't Seth have a gun? At least at the house they could call the police.

Breathing evenly, Everett calmed himself as he thought through the plan.

Then suddenly, Chuck's voice seemed to shriek in his mind, *YELLOW BELLY!* Everett gritted his teeth and shook it off. He had to be like D.G. He had to think like D.G. He wasn't going to run.

The station wagon sat far down underneath them. Everett figured they were more than fifteen feet up.

Tina whispered, "They're screaming at them now. What if they hurt D.G. or Linc?"

The hair tingled on Everett's neck. *YELLOW BELLY!*

He punched the edge of the window, then said, "Okay. Don't worry. We'll get them out of this." Saying it out loud seemed to strengthen him.

He quickly tied the belts into a beam by the window. The pipe bent up toward the roof, then ran straight into the ground. He could hold onto the belts most of the way down the side. But could Tina do it? Could he do it? He didn't know. They had to. They had to get Seth and the police. That was all he could think about.

"I'm going out. Soon as I get down, you come."

She nodded her eyes glistened with tears. He began to

back himself out the hole.

It was difficult getting into position to grab the pipe, but with the help of the belts, he made it. He jammed his fingers around the pipe, held onto the belt and slowly let himself down, bracing his sneakers against the side of the building. He let himself down quickly, silently.

When he reached the end of the belts, he let go and dropped. Six feet!

His knees whammed up into his chest. The wind was knocked out of him, but he was on the ground. He stood there against the side of the building, praying that no one would come and see them. It seemed that Tina waited hours before she appeared at the edge, but then her legs dangled out. Everett held his breath as he watched, standing underneath, ready to catch her if necessary.

She inched down. When she reached the end of the belts, she glanced down at him, a terrified look on her face. Then she dropped.

She fell into his arms and slid through. She hardly bent her knees. When she turned around she was trembling. "How are we going to get Linc and D.G. out?"

Everett grabbed her hand. "We'll figure that out. Come on."

His heart banged away, but he reviewed the plan. He said, "We'll go deep into the woods behind and catch the road down a ways. We can't let them see us, or they might do something to Linc and D.G. Then we find Seth. He'll know what to do."

Tina nodded, biting her lip. He felt her hand at his back

as they scurried around the station wagon. A moment later, she gasped, "They left the keys in the car."

Everett looked in. "Good, that might help." He might be able to start it or something. That might scare them out of the house. But how could he do it? He'd never started a car before. Still, he'd seen his dad do it hundreds of times. You turned the key, you pressed the gas. Then you had to take it out of gear. He hoped it wouldn't come to that.

In front of the car, the yard behind the house sloped to the woods about a hundred feet away. He figured he could drive the car into the trees, then run.

Then: *No. Not yet. We have to get to Seth's first.*

Everett told himself again, *Think like an Israeli! Think like D.G.*

Leaving the car behind, they sped into the woods, trying to keep as quiet as they could. Everett grabbed Tina's hand and pulled her behind him. No one came around the edge of the house. Once they got Seth he was sure it would all be okay.

They dashed through the woods until they saw the dirt road to Seth's house. Then Everett let go of Tina's hand, and they raced down the road. *Seth has to be there*, Everett prayed in his mind. *He just has to.*

But when they reached the house, Seth's truck was gone. Everett's heart sank. Whip and Bump jumped up and ran out to greet them. He patted the dogs' heads and called out, "Seth! Seth!"

There was no answer. Everett knew he must have been

around earlier, or the dogs would not have been off their chains. Tina said, "Seth gets home around 3:30, right?"

Everett nodded and looked around.

Tina said again, "Everett, how are we going to get them out? We've got to get going!"

Everett tried Seth's door, but it was locked. He couldn't even call the police. Then he noticed a piece of chalk lying on the ground. Seth used it to mark off his roses.

Ideas flooding his mind, Everett picked up the chalk. He said to Tina, "I'll write a message for Seth on the house and hope he gets home in a few minutes. It's got to be past three by now."

He wrote in huge letters on the side of the house. "Get the police. Come to the abandoned house down the road to the left, driveway on the right. D.G. and Linc and others held by . . ."

"Thugs!" said Tina with finality. She stood there, hugging herself, her eyes narrow and angry now. Her jaw was set.

Everett wrote it.

Finishing, he searched with his eyes, desperate for any idea. Whip and Bump stood in front of them, wagging their tails. Maybe they could help. He said, "All right, we'll take Whip and Bump and go back. If we have to, we'll sic Whip and Bump on them. They'll obey you, right?"

Tina nodded, "I think so."

He spotted the green wire lying on the ground that Seth also used for his roses. He picked it up. He wasn't sure for what, but some vague ideas came into his head about tripping the thieves.

"Okay, let's go and pray Seth gets here and gets the cops!" He flickered a smile. Tina's lips pursed and her face twitched. But he patted her on the back and assured her, "It'll be okay. We'll get them out. All of them."

She nodded, her eyes blinking with fear.

Already a plan was forming in Everett's head. They raced down the road with Whip and Bump beside them. *Just get to that car. Just get the car!*

Their breath came hard, but they didn't slow down. Whip and Bump bounced along beside them, looking for the world like they were going to the beach. On the way, Everett noticed nice, round stones in the road and stopped to pick them up and jam them into his pocket. He might have to use his slingshot.

His heart was thundering.

Tina kept looking at him. "You don't think they'd hurt them, do you?"

He answered grimly, "We're going to get them out. No matter what." He tried to sound certain. Like D.G.

24
Think like an Israeli

Plans flashed through Everett's mind as he ran. He discarded some, but slowly a whole course of action came together in his mind. By the time they reached the top of the road, he had a clear idea of what to do. They crept off into the woods and advanced to a spot right before the metal posts. When they stopped, Everett listened intently.

Above the panting of the dogs, they heard the two older men swearing loudly in the house. Then D.G.'s voice: "We weren't doing anything. Just exploring." There was a pause, and then D.G. cried out, "You have no right to do that!"

Everett heard Chuck and Stuart also cry out in pain. He

glanced at Tina and quickly explained what he planned to do. She listened and nodded hopefully. "I'll do whatever you say," she told him.

As she waited in the woods with Whip and Bump, he strung the wire between the two metal posts, keeping low so as not to be seen. He secured it back and forth two times. He didn't know if that would hold the car, or anything else, but he thought it might slow somebody up. It was a "just in case" kind of thing. But he had a gut feeling about it. The green wire was hard to see until you were right on it. That was good.

He turned and looked at Tina. "It's going to work," she mouthed and gave him a thumbs up.

He whispered to her, "If one of them comes after me, sic Whip and Bump on them. But be careful."

The sunlight was hot on his back. He didn't know what time it was, but he was sure it was well past 3:30 now. Where were Seth and the police?

Taking another deep breath, he took off into the woods. He prayed the keys were still in the car. When he came out on the opposite side, he could hear the two older men arguing between themselves.

"That's murder, Jack. We can't do that."

"Then what do you say?"

"Just tie them up and lock them in the cellar until we can get out of here. They wouldn't be found for days."

"But they know who we are."

The other man swore.

"You never should have let your little brother in on this," Jack yelled. "They know about the electronic equipment, too, man. We can't leave them here to tell the FBI or something."

Everett swallowed. What on earth were they going to do? Surely they weren't going to kill them! *Just get going*, an inner voice said.

He edged up to the car and looked in. The keys were still in it. Opening the door on the right side, he crawled in, leaving the door open a crack. He didn't want to make any unnecessary noises. The back was crammed with the electronic equipment.

Everett slid over into the driver's seat. What now? Well, what did his dad do? He tried to reach the gas pedal with his foot. Was it that far? He slid under the steering column and pressed it with his toe. But how could he start it, put it in gear, and jump out all at once? This was harder than he'd thought.

"Okay, put the car in gear," he murmured. Then the lever wouldn't move. What was wrong? "Think like an Israeli. Think like D.G.," he muttered again, looking around.

What did his father do? That was it! The ignition key had to be turned on before you could put it in gear. He twisted the key.

The engine jolted, nearly knocking him over with fright.

Nothing else happened though, and he recovered.

"Okay, press the gas," he said. "Then the key, put it in gear, and jump out."

He turned the key and pressed on the gas. The steering wheel was right under his chin. He couldn't even see where it was going. The engine roared. He dropped back on the gas, and the machine began to idle.

It was now or never. He pulled the shift lever back, then slammed it all the way down. The engine almost died, but then the car inched forward.

Get out!

He ripped at the handle to his left. The door didn't open. What was wrong? He cranked on the door again. Nothing moved. The car clunked over some stones, and the long grass in the backyard swished under it. It was picking up speed.

What was wrong?

Someone shouted behind him: "Get that kid!"

The car jerked and swayed over the stones in the backyard. It was heading straight for the trees. But how could he get out?

The other side. Get out the other side, something screamed in his head. He slid over. With one quick move, he kicked the door open and rolled out onto the ground. He looked up as the car kept going.

Immediately, he saw the two thieves now, with little O'Brien, sprinting like madmen to catch the car. The one named Dan had a knife out and veered off toward Everett.

Everett jumped up. *RUN! Now, for Tina and the dogs.*

"You get the car!" shouted the one named Dan. "I'll get the kid." Jack and little O'Brien sped after the car.

His thighs aching, Everett pumped his legs as hard as he could. He had to get past the posts. That was his only chance.

The knife up, Dan barreled after him. "Stop, kid! You're dead meat!"

Everett pushed his legs even faster. The big man's footsteps thudded behind him. He was getting closer.

Just reach the posts! Don't look back!

"I'll throw the knife," the man yelled, his breath coming hard. Everett's arms flailed at the air and he pumped his legs even faster. Everything looked blurry.

"I'm gonna throw it!"

"No way I'm stopping," Everett yelled. His lungs burned as he zigzagged slightly, not wanting to give Dan a clear throw.

The posts were only forty feet ahead. He could just see the wire. Did Dan see the wire? His lungs screamed for air.

The boots seemed so loud behind him, Everett thought any moment the big hand would yank him down.

It was just another fifteen feet. If Dan went between them and hit the wire, maybe . . .

The moment Everett reeled past the posts, he dug in even harder with a final spurt. Then he glanced back. Dan ran straight toward the wire. He had the knife in his right hand. He was cursing now and screaming at Everett.

It was working. But where were Tina and the dogs?

Then he saw them in the trees. Tina's eyes were wide with fright, but he could see she was steady as steel.

Everett burned up the road. If Dan was going to hit the wire, he'd hit it now. . . .

"YOW!" The big thug fell headlong, tumbling and rolling. Everett skidded to a halt and spun around.

Tina screamed, "Get him!"

Instantly, Whip and Bump bounded out. They pounced on Dan growling and barking furiously, their white teeth flashing in the light. Whip bit into a foot and Bump had a hand. Dan screamed, "Get off me! Call your dogs off."

Breathing hard, Everett bent over. Then he spotted the knife in the middle of the road. He staggered over, picked it up, and threw it into the woods. The dogs held the man by the foot and arm, shaking him in their teeth. Dan screamed and cursed, trying to ball up, but it didn't help.

Looking up, Everett saw the car stopped behind the house. "Watch him! Don't let him go!" He shouted to Tina.

She stood on the edge of the woods yelling at Whip and Bump to "bite the thug!" The two dogs were good. Everett grinned to himself. *That was for sure.*

25
Out!

Satisfied that Tina had the situation under control, Everett raced back to the house. Where were little O'Brien and Jack? And D.G. and Linc? When he reached the side of the house, he peeked around. He could still see the car down the hill, almost in the trees. He heard the engine turning over.

Everett pulled out his slingshot and a stone. Where was Seth? And where were the police? Where on earth were the police?

He hurried into the house. "D.G.! Linc!"

Stopping to listen, he heard muffled voices at the

back part of the house. "We're here. In the cellar."

Everett dashed back to the kitchen. The latch was on with the padlock, but the padlock hadn't been pushed in. He jerked it off. The door popped open.

"Man are we glad . . ." D.G. shouted. His eye was bruised, and Linc's lip was cut, but they were smiling.

Everett didn't give them time to talk. "Come on. Get your slingshot. O'Brien and Jack are still loose." Chuck and Stuart came up behind them, looking angry and ready to run. Everett said to them, "You guys can throw stones at them."

But Chuck pushed past them. "I'm outta here, man."

He and Stuart ran out the front door toward the woods. "That figures," D.G. said.

As they stepped out onto the stoop, Tina was running toward them, gesturing wildly. "They're coming back up the hill!"

Everett pulled three stones out of his pocket. "Linc, D.G., use your slings. There're more stones in the driveway. Come on."

As Chuck and Stuart disappeared into the woods in front of the house. Everett bounded around the house with D.G., Linc, and Tina following. He yelled, "Let's give it to them."

Tina picked up some stones from the driveway. Jack and little O'Brien stalked up the hill toward them.

"Stop!" shouted Everett, beginning to whirl his sling.

Swearing, Jack came at them, crouching down. He also

had a knife. Little O'Brien swung a chain in his hand and had a mean grin pasted on his lips.

"Give it to them," shouted Everett. He and D.G. whirled their slings harder. Linc and Tina readied to throw their stones.

The four stones smacked the two in the legs and chest. Jack ducked down and stopped, swearing at them again. Tina and Linc threw more stones at little O'Brien while D.G. and Everett set new stones in their sling pouches.

Jack jumped up, snarling. But he hesitated and little O'Brien looked at him, as if they weren't sure whether to run back or forward. D.G. let another stone fly. Jack moved out of the way just as it whizzed by his temple. Everett, Linc, and Tina all fired at the same time.

The shots were true, striking them again in the legs and arms.

Jack spun around. "I'm going for the car."

Little O'Brien ducked his head, crimson with rage. "I can take you all," he roared. He ran toward the foursome, whipping the chain sideways in his hand.

Everett hesitated, but just a moment. "Hit him! Gang tackle!" he yelled and he and D.G. bolted forward. Tina threw another rock, striking O'Brien in the thigh, then she and Linc leapt forward behind D.G. and Everett.

O'Brien tried to hit Everett with the chain, but Everett ducked in time and tackled him at the waist. A moment later, D.G. grabbed a leg. O'Brien pitched over them, smacking down into the dirt. He screamed in pain. The chain clattered to the ground in front of him.

On the ground, O'Brien tried to roll over, but Everett and D.G. pounced on top of him. They wrestled his arm around behind his back until they had him pinned face downward. Linc and Tina piled on, holding his legs down. The notebook was folded in half in his back pocket. Everett pulled it out and threw it onto the ground.

Then they heard the car. Everett turned around and saw Chuck and Stuart standing by the corner of the house. He shouted, "Throw rocks at the car. Keep him in it."

But neither boy moved.

The engine roared as Jack made the wheels spin. The vehicle bounced and jolted in place. It was obviously lodged on a rock or stump. Everett held his breath. O'Brien pitched and tried to roll but he and D.G. gripped him tightly. He began swearing. D.G. yelled and cuffed his ear. "We'll break your arm if you keep moving!"

Suddenly, the car shot out backward with a scraping crunch. It veered to the left and began to turn around. In a moment, Everett knew they'd be done for.

He screamed at Chuck, "Throw stones at it. Do something."

Chuck didn't move.

"We've got to get out of here," Linc yelled through clenched teeth.

"Pull O'Brien to his feet," Everett shouted.

O'Brien tried to throw them off. But he realized they couldn't let him up. He'd tear them to pieces.

The car began to turn now, ready to drive at them.

There was no chance.

Everett closed his eyes. "Please, God . . . "

Then they heard the sirens. Three police cars, lights flashing and sirens blaring, crashed through the wire at the posts. The first car roared past the four on O'Brien, came up in front of Jack's car, and skidded sideways to a stop. Before Jack could jump out, the policemen were at his window with guns drawn.

Moments later, it seemed as though there were police all over the place. One took little O'Brien from the foursome and handcuffed him.

Everett, still shaking, stood with D.G., Linc, and Tina. For a moment, they were all silent as they watched the thugs being led away. Then Tina burst into tears, Linc hugged her, Everett put his arms around both of them, and D.G. yelled, "Bold!" They held one another, sobbing and encouraging each other until Seth ran up, his eyes wide and worried.

"What on earth happened with you kids?" Seth cried. They all turned to him, and he enveloped them in his brawny arms. "Lord, what's the world doin' to itself?" But soon the tears were gone and Whip and Bump trotted about, sniffing the policemen and watching the action.

"Should we show them their tricks?" Tina asked as she dried her eyes.

Seth smiled and patted her shoulder. "We've seen enough tricks for one day." He looked around at the four earnest faces. "That was one piece of work," Seth said, shaking his head. "How did you do it?"

"Everett did it," Tina said.

Everett shook his head. "We all did it," he said. But everyone gazed at him with awe and joy in their eyes.

D.G. said, "They were talking about cutting our throats. They really were."

Everett grinned, shifting his weight and fingering the slingshot in his hand. He had never felt happier. Something began to gush and squirm inside him, and he wanted to scream for joy. He felt so proud to be friends with D.G., Linc, Tina—Seth, too, and Whip and Bump. They were better than he ever could have asked for.

Then as Everett quietly petted the dogs, Seth stooped down in front of Everett and fixed him with stern but kind eyes. "I hope you know the good Lord was with you this afternoon, boy."

"I know," Everett said.

"He was thinking like David did with Goliath," D.G. added.

Everyone laughed.

The policemen checked out the house and found a huge stash of electronic equipment in the basement. Several of them took down Everett's and the others' stories. One of them told Everett they'd been looking for this ring of thieves for months.

As Everett listened and enjoyed the compliments and encouragement, he thought of what his mother said about

God giving him a second chance. He wondered if this was God's answer to that prayer. Then suddenly he knew it was and he said quietly, *Thanks*.

Finally, things began to wind down and the kids watched as the police made a final cleanup and drove the three thieves away in one of the cars. It was then that Everett noticed the little black-and-white-flecked notebook on the ground. He stooped and picked it up. As he looked up, he saw Chuck staring at him uneasily.

The moment their eyes met, Everett knew he wasn't afraid of Chuck anymore. He didn't want to see Chuck hurt or put down or even disliked. He just wanted the whole thing to end. But he also knew something had been proved, something he could never prove by trying to beat Chuck in a fight.

Everett swallowed and his eyes burned for a moment. Then he noticed D.G. tugging at his shirt. "Come on, we get to ride in a cop car."

Everett nodded. "Wait a minute."

He walked over to Chuck and held out the book. "This wasn't right, Chuck. You can have it. I'm sorry I told them some of your secrets."

Chuck took the book, but he wouldn't look Everett in the eye. As he started to climb into the police car, he suddenly turned to Everett. "Why don't you ride with us?"

Everett's heart seemed to stop. He saw D.G. standing in the doorway of the next car up, waving him to hurry. He looked back at Chuck's drawn, tired face. "Thanks, but I'll

ride in the other car." He didn't have to say, "With D.G.,
Linc, and Tina."

Chuck shrugged and got in.

A moment later, Everett plopped into the backseat of
the second police car next to D.G. Tina and Linc were
already nestled in the corner. D.G. said triumphantly,
"We're famous now, guys! There're going to be reporters
and everything."

But Everett simply sat back and enjoyed the banter.
Seth eased into the front seat with Whip, and Bump
crawled into the back on Tina's and Linc's laps.

"So how's it feel to be a hero?" D.G. said to Everett.

Everett smiled sheepishly. "I don't think so, D.G."

"You came up with the plan," Tina said. "You should get
a medal!"

"Yeah, but you got the dogs on the first guy," Everett
answered. "And we all got O'Brien."

Seth turned around. "I think I need my camera for this
one."

Then D.G. said with finality, "Well, I'm going to tell
them you saved my life."

"Me, too," said Linc. Bump barked.

Everyone laughed, and as they headed down the
driveway, D.G. suddenly gestured toward the woods.
"Anyway, enough of this hero stuff. Tomorrow we find the
trees."

Linc, Tina, and Everett all said at the same time, "The
trees?"

"For the tree fort," D.G. said. "Fort Dayan, after Moshe. It'll be the greatest. We'll build it in the woods. We just have to find four trees together in a square." He looked from Everett to Linc and Tina with that confident glow in his eyes that Everett had seen a thousand times.

For a moment, Everett chuckled inside. It was perfect D.G. all the way—already thinking a million miles ahead of everyone else. Well, that was the way he was, and as far as Everett was concerned, D.G. should keep on being that way for as long as he lived.

Be sure to read about Everett, D.G., Linc, and Tina in the next

Rocky Creek Adventure

What could be better than building a tree fort, playing along the creek bank, and exploring hidden caves? The summer would have been perfect if Chuck and his gang hadn't reappeared. . . .

"Hey, Scarface!"

D.G. shot up and fixed his eyes on Chuck. Everyone scrambled to their feet. Everett dropped down to the first floor of the tree fort and retrieved his slingshot. On the ground in seconds, D.G. straddled a log in front of the tree fort. Everett followed. "What do you want, Chuck?" D.G. asked.

"Who do you think you are, building a tree house in these woods?" called Chuck. "These are our woods."

Anger gripped Everett's stomach, but D.G. simply said, "Right, and I suppose Tina's pool is your pool and the United States government is . . . "

"Don't go sassing me," Chuck answered. "I'll bust you quick, Scarface." The other boys with him laughed.

"Chuck, why can't we just get along?" D.G. said suddenly. "You could build your own tree fort down here if . . ."

"Don't want a tree fort," said Chuck, and spit on the ground in front of D.G.

After a moment's hesitation, Everett hurried over to D.G. He thought maybe he could yank him back to safety.

"Look," D.G. said with a shrug, "you want to make a deal, let's make a deal. We don't have to be nasty to each . . . "

Spitting again, Chuck said, "I'll be any way I want with you. Got it, Frankl?"